"Those who play with the devil's toys will be brought by degrees to wield his sword."

— R. Buckminster Fuller

MorbidbookS is a grotesque Bizarro ballet where the most profane things occur. An impious and perverse dwelling of dark revulsion. A cozy cottage where torture porn and brutal bible tales are devised. A quiet place to relax and spin tales of depravity and wickedness. A halfway house for the disturbed where rules no longer apply.  A safe haven for deviant serial killers to hatch their wretched schemes.

Bring your pets.

The tasty ones are always welcome.

WWW.MORBIDBOOKS.WORDPRESS.COM

# BRIAN THE MAKER

By Gregor Cole

For

# 1.

IF BRIAN WAS to get pulled over now, his life would be over.

He had no clue where he was going or what he would do when he got there and by now the authorities would have broken the door down to his basement flat and found the collection of necrotized fuck toys he had sculpted.

Several of these artefacts had orifices crudely sewn up with copper wire and others holes cut into them for sexual gratification. He took pleasure in his hobby, his craft and was not ready to be stopped just yet.

Brian hadn't realized it at the time but he had gone quite mad; he must have done, otherwise he wouldn't have completed all that stuff with the shit and blood and the guts. No, he would be having a cup of tea at home watching the telly not driving into the night with a woman's head on the floor of his car.

He looked down into the foot well of the passenger seat, a woman's face looked up at him. It wasn't so much a human head anymore, more the face of one of those cheap plastic sex dolls you'd find in a student house for cheap laughs.

Painted up to look pretty yet looking worse for it with mouth in a big 'O', eyelids stretched and pinned back with a startled, constant look of surprise. A look more of horror that pleasure.

Brian liked that look; the cheap, shocked look.

The whole thing arranged with a layer of plastic wrap, clear tape and fish hooks. Her green eyes dull under the plastic and her blond hair now pinkish from the struggle and the sharp blow to the back of her skull that landed her here.

Well, at least landing her head here, staring up at this monstrous pervert.

Brian was slightly glad it was the middle of the night with the weather slowly turning to shit; heavy rain made him harder to spot through misty, streaked glass even for eagle-eyed policemen.

On nights like this Brian suspected that the pigs would have their hands full taking turns wanking each other off in a lay-by somewhere; or perhaps beating up some crack whore before raping her and taking all her drugs to sell in the canteen back at the station.

Brian was more of the sceptical type.

At some point he would have to ditch the car someplace, find an alternative route, alternate means of travel. He had already driven some distance and hoped that the police hadn't thought to plan this far ahead; as long as he kept his speed down it'd be smooth sailing, but to where?

Maybe they hadn't even found his collection; his pieces still sitting there, holes forced open and pre-lubed, waiting, wanting him to fill them with himself and whatever came to hand.

Wine bottle, knife, hacksaw, cricket bat, the next door neighbour's pet cat Winston, whatever came to hand. He had felt a little bad for killing the cat; he had never intended to fuck a corpse with a live animal. It just sort of happened. When the inquisitive creature had sneaked into his the flat and sniffed at Brian's balls mid-coitus. Brian wasn't even thinking straight when he jammed the moggy's head first into the bored open fuck hole.

Poor old Wilson, the fluffy little bastard.

Brian tried to remember how all this started as he drove into the torrential night; it almost hurt his head trying to recall the events leading to this moment in time.

Maybe it had started when he was at university.

He had a girlfriend in his final year that had gotten him into some weird stuff sexually then she left him for a guy with a bigger cock. The other guy was some gay looking chump with muscles and a tattoo; the pair had died in a car accident and Brian took a dump on their graves after each of their funerals.

Fuck the both of them.

But after she had left him he needed to fill the void of the newfound enjoyment of sickening sexual practices.

Brain had purchased one of those 'real life' sex dolls online from a Japanese company; the company had some kooky name like 'FUKARADA' or something. Crazy Japanese bastards, they really led the way in the perverse.

Boy did the thing look real; you could bend it into any position and it came armed with enormous tits, willing mouth and a supposedly real feel pussy and anus. The packaging said to 'just add lubricant' but there was a problem. There was something missing; the smells, the tastes and the feel of real skin.

You can't emulate that.

So Brian set out to attempt to build a real life sex toy made from real life people.

In the coming months he studied religiously anything and everything concerning taxidermy, furniture restoration, skin preservation and tanning, basic robotics and anything he could find on the perversities of man.

Greek text, German literature, old manuscripts from the Far East and India describing bizarre sex acts that bordered on torture.

He started to attend sex addiction meetings just to gain inspiration from some of the addict's stories. Most times he would pass on the opportunity to speak and when he did he was usually asked to leave the group.

Brian had captured a girl from a group meeting on sexual health and tortured her, masturbating over her bruised and battered face as she choked on her teeth. After killing her, by accident because he had hit her too hard, he trussed her up and used lengths of bamboo cane to fix her into poses. This way he could manipulate her into different positions just like his old rubber companion but with the added bonus of the thing being human.

It was after his third attempt at the perfect fuck toy that he discovered that he could put the canes inside the flesh of the girl's arms and legs again just like his Japanese rubber girlfriend. He also found that using thick wire mesh wrapped around the joints could hold them into position for longer. The mesh was also good for holding in the organs if he ever got a little carried away with himself, which was often.

Poor old Winston.

It was around this point that he started to become creative, letting go of his inner pervert and giving way to his darkest fantasies.

Brian had stitched two girls together, back to back and removed their legs at the hips and their heads. He then turned them upside-down and placed their arms out like the legs found on a plant stand. Brian now had himself a four-holed fuck-toy. You just walked up to it like a urinal and picked a hole. Then you just stuffed your dick in and away you went.

He had enjoyed it for several days before some of the holes had become over bruised and had started to turn into a slushy pulp.

Brian kept that in the bathroom now with a large money plant perched on top of it.

And now he was here, running from the police that to be fair might not even be looking for him.

It occurred to Brian that he might just be running from his own paranoia; after all he did have a girl's severed head with him in the car. He was toying with the idea of pulling off into one of the country road and mouth fucking his ride along companion, but he was too afraid of being caught in a policeman's torch light.

How could he explain that one? It would be bad enough getting caught fucking a live girl.

He would have to find a motel off the beaten track, somewhere to hide for a few days.

Brian would have to lose the car too.

## 2.

MRS. SAQQAF HAD called the police after Brian had just upped and left in his car.

He had looked panicked and drove away at great speed; he wasn't carrying much in the way of luggage, a large hold-all over his shoulder and what looked like a football under his arm.

She had a key to the flat, but didn't want to go down there on her own; it hadn't been the same since her husband had died, she was a little apprehensive and called the police.

She had heard odd noises of late coming from down there. Sex noise, machine noise, violent noise.

But it was the smell that had caused the most alarm.

It had started to come up through the floor several weeks before Brian did his midnight flit. That paired with the weird sounds coming from Brian's rooms only heightened suspicion.

This is why Mrs Saqqaf was waiting for the police. She had no intention on walking in there without big, burly policemen in front of her.

The police car arrived around 4pm, and the officers took the keys from Mrs Saqqaf and she explained about the smell and the sounds and how the tenant had fled in the night at high speed. They wrote down a statement and headed down the concrete stairs to where Brian had once resided.

The smell was heavy as the opened the door; the thick, sickly sweet scent of putrefaction.

One of the officers threw his partner a knowing look and they entered with caution to be met with what looked like at first glance quite a normal living room.

TV, coffee table, bookshelves, X-box, stereo cabinet, sofa... ah, the sofa. There was something amiss about the sofa, something odd. It was covered with a large Indian throw over, decorated with a print of a multi-armed Asian goddess. The goddess played a flute with one set of arms, was slaughtering a lamb with another and ripping an infant child into pieces above her head with another set.

But it wasn't the throw that was amiss, the sofa underneath was more than it seemed, it was just a little odd.

The officer nearest the sofa took a corner of the throw and whipped it back. They both stood agog in shock at what was underneath.

A mass if tangled limbs and metal rods fashioned into the shape of a large two seater couch. Hands and feet planted firmly to the floor, butchered rows of thighs as seat cushions and severed arms upright as back support. The thick wire stitching and mesh were holding everything together.

There were also two severed heads, eyes and mouths sealed with red wax and arranged like scatter cushions in each corner of the macabre couch.

"Fuck sake is this thing real, Mark?" The first officer looked at his partner in shocked awe.

"I'm calling this in. This is fucking rough." The second officer's radio crackled into life.

It seemed like a matter of moments before the house was crawling with forensics officers bathed in bright flood lights intermixed with the flashes of blue and the pitched bleep of radios. Officers buzzed around, tapping off this and sealing off that; holding back the crowd of neighbours that had started to accumulate outside. A visual barrier of yellow tape assisted in keeping them at bay. The sound of an officer vomiting down in the entrance to the flat could be heard over the clamour of police work.

Men wearing dust masks and white full body suits hauled out heavy black rubber bags to waiting private ambulances.

A skinny, pigeon like man in a white overall covering his cheap suit jotted down notes and ID numbers from the bag tags on a clipboard. He stopped every now and then to shake his pen or push up his glasses. He was constantly on edge; his eyes darted from black bag to officer, from forensics to the ambulances.

He tapped his pen on the top of the clipboard to the beat of some tune that floated around his head, his internal radio; the radio somehow always got stuck on some cheesy 80's station.

"Don't save a prayer for me now...." he mumbled under his breath in an off key.

Another black bag, this time the shape of a pyramid was presented to him. He glanced at the tag and jotted the number.

"Where was it?" He asked.

"It was the kitchen. We found some kind of wine rack made of arms and shit," was the reply through a white dust mask from an officer.

"Wine, eh? No doubt those bottles will make their way into the staff canteen down at the morgue, hah!" He raised an eyebrow to the man in the mask and waited for a laugh in reply... it didn't come.

"Whatever, mate." The officer lugged the bag back up to his chest, and trudged towards one of the privet ambulances. He threw it in the back with the several other bags now piling up that had been just tossed in like junk mail sacks.

He took out a packet of cigarettes from his pocket and made his way towards a makeshift buffet table that was an old bit of wood and a few beer crates that had been knocked together by some of the WPC's.

One of the locals had made a shit load of sandwiches and left them for the officers to dive into. The officer thumbed through a row of egg and cress and felt his gag reflex twitch. He would rather be down in the flat filled with body parts that eat a fucking egg sandwich.

But there was coffee. Coffee was a good thing.

He pulled the mask over his head and the hood of his dust suit with it to reveal the face of detective Simon Jennings.

He poured a cup of lukewarm dark liquid into a standard issue white polystyrene cup that put his teeth on edge a little as one of his canine teeth bumped on the cheap cup as he sipped from it; lit his cigarette and slowly strolled behind the makeshift canteen.

"So, we like to make things out of young girls do we," he said under his breath, exhaling a thick line of smoke into the air, "Well then, better find you pretty fast my old chum."

He sighed and flopped down into a plastic patio chair left from a barbeque party on the pavement.

It was going to be a long night.

# 3.

BRIAN SAT IN the darkness of his car, parked up in a quiet corner of a drive thru looking down at the severed head in his lap.

A half-eaten cheese burger was cooling alone and forlorn on the dashboard.

He was in awe of the thing he had made sitting on the floor of the car. Some of the tape had started to fray at the edges and the skin being pulled back by one of the fish hooks had started to tear away. The mouth had sunk in slightly in places through over use.

She was starting to look worse for wear.

He slurped at his drink and looked out into the night. The authorities must be aware of his crimes by now.

The door of his flat would be off the hinges and his place would be crawling with police and forensic specialists like a fucked up episode of CSI Miami. Brian loved that show. He liked the one with Ted Danson in it but only really for Ted Danson.

"Hope they don't mess up the carpet," was the only thing he could say as he took another swig from the wax paper covered beverage.

Brian dropped the head back into the foot well of the passenger seat and turned the ignition key. The engine coughed into life and he revved the engine slightly to warm it up.

He still had no idea where he would go, or how far he would get.

Brian didn't want to be caught; he had so much still to do but he feared that it was only a matter of days before he would be picked up. He would have to give them one last thing to see, one last great piece of art for the boffins to analyse, something that would launch him into super-infamy. It would have to be special; something that would make every front page in ever paper on every café table across the land.

He pulled out into the slowly dwindling, post-midnight traffic and the heavy rain of the failing summer. Brian would have to find some kind of base, a place to finish the game. One that was public enough to go unseen and not arouse any undue suspicion. He would also need some supplies, including a selection of girls for his grisly works. But it would need to be just off the beaten track and hard to find.

Then he remembered a place he had gone to with his ex-girlfriend, a motel that had bungalows by a small lake.

It had been a romantic weekend; they had walked by the water and fed the ducks. Enjoyed a candlelit meal in the five star restaurant and she had tied him up and stuffed her panties in his mouth before roughly beating and fucking him in the king leisure bed.

Yes, it would have to be there; it was as good as perfect.

He drove through the night, the severed felatio toy in the foot well rolling and bumping about and the smell of the cheese burger still hanging in the car.

A small boy had looked at it from the window of a high SUV when he had stopped for petrol and a grot mag, but the look on the child's face told him that the boy wasn't going to tell anyone.

Brian had remembered the route to the motel perfectly, but it had brought back several memories of the rocky relationship with his ex; all the rows, the violence, and the tolerance to horrific sexual torture that she had.

He remembered the time she had told him she had cheated on him. It was not with just one guy but with two at the same time. And then she proceeded to explain to Brian how she would have wanted him to see her getting destroyed by the men.

She had seen that as some kind of foreplay, he was shocked and felt nauseous at the news but fucked her anyway.

He pulled into the drive and was delighted that the place hadn't changed. It was just as he remembered. There was the faux Americana of the place, the pines in the drive and the cut logs lined up outside for the wood burning open fire pit in the restaurant area.

It had the look of a ski lodge, the kind you'd find in the mountains of Switzerland, not by some manmade lake off the motorway. But there was still something a little plastic about the place, something false.

It was trying to be something that had no place in that location or even in that era. It was a throwback to everything that was horrid about the 70's.

Brian carefully wrapped his fuck toy in some newspaper and an oily rag he had in the boot of his car. He then placed the thing in an off-licence carrier bag, a blue and white stripped thing; thin enough to just make out the shape of a head, but it could be a melon from a passing glance.

He stuffed it into the holdall containing his cloths and a can of lynx voodoo deodorant.

Then he climbed the front stairs and swung the heavy doors open into the foyer. He would have to play it cool. Act confident, he couldn't afford to show his nervousness. Brian would have to play it cool.

The place smelt of stale beer and disinfectant and was the colour of shame. That grotty orange and brown décor that he remembered from the last time he was here. For some reason all he could think of was some low budget soap opera.

The girl on the front desk was all smiles and cleavage, her blond hair tied back tight in a bun on the back of her head. The top button of her shirt was open, on purpose, making her seem more accessible.

She wore a small gold pendant that read 'Juicy' in swirled lettering. He wanted to put the pendant inside part of her then fuck her so deep with it that it would be hard to find again. Brian shook the thought off and smiled back at her.

He had seen a documentary on how retail and hoteliers train their staff to flirt and dress with a touch of trash to keep their customers comfortable and happy. A happy customer is a regular customer.

But for Brian, he saw things a little different. He saw himself playing hacky-sack with one of her tits, sewn up tight like a small bean bag. Maybe drill a gaping hole in her stomach for him to pleasure himself with and a stool made from her buttocks.

Brian looked back at the pendant, then back at the girl. The smile was getting harder to maintain.

With a quick signature and a fake name Brian booked into the last free bungalow by the lake.

He strolled with his bag over his shoulder down the leaf littered walkway to the door, room 112. It was the room from his past stay.

A flash of his ex, taking a shit on his chest burst into his head and he remembered how powerless he was, cable tied to the bed posts. He gritted his teeth and fought the memories from his mind.

Brian looked both ways down the walkway checking for anything before he shut the door, locked it and slid the latch across.

He placed his bag on the coffee table in the centre of the room and sat on the long two seater sofa.

Slowly, he unzipped the bag; the faint smell of rot filled his nostrils as he pulled the head from the holdall and un-wrapped the thing.

He stared at it.

It stared back with its dull green eyes and expression of surprise.

"We have a lot of preparation to consider you and me."

He picked up the head and kissed it deeply on the mouth then threw his makeshift companion on the bed.

Brian felt a twitch in his trousers.

# 4.

SALLY WALKED DOWN the bland corridor past fake plants and across maroon wall to wall carpeting.

One of the wheels of the shitty cleaning trolley squeaked a little as she pushed it down the hall. The smell of the horrid blue hi-phosphate toilet cleaner stinging in her nostrils; the smell always made her feel a bit sick.

She had taken the job to pay for her tuition but had to drop out of collage due to her unplanned pregnancy. She still had no idea who the father was but had narrowed it down to about three different guys.

If only she had listened to her mother.

"You'll end up in some dump working for shit, letting dirty blokes have their way with you, you daft cow." Sally shuddered hearing her mum's voice in her head, but she was right in her own mad as hell way.

Sally's mum killed herself in a mental hospital and was buried in a potter's field on the institute's grounds on the free. Sally didn't go to the funeral.

"Room 123, 145, 147 and chalet 112, what a fucking top night," she sighed to herself and continued pushing the shoddy trolley. There had been a stag party staying the night before so a few of the rooms needed that extra special treatment; that woman's touch.

"That's why you' on the big money my girl." She chuckled to herself; it was a way of stopping the tears from coming.

Most of the toilets needed a good scrubbing. Shit, puke, spunk and blood covered most everything in the bathrooms. One of the showers had a Jonny blocking the plughole so that it has flooded. She had found two unopened bottles of champagne, a gram of cocaine and forty cigarettes which she stashed in away in the trolley.

"Every cloud and all that," she muttered to herself.

All of the sheets from the stag party's room needed the laundry; a good fucking boil-wash to get rid of two days of filth and debauchery.

It's amazing how many of these rugby types just shit themselves in the night on these away weekend things. One of them had fallen asleep in a quiet spot in the lobby wearing nothing but a bed sheet and a single rubber glove. The hotel staff was only made aware of his presence when they heard him violently throw up into one of the potted plastic ferns.

He was billed for the mess and asked to go back to his room. He was later found out by the lake covered in his own shit singing a Van Morrison song. The police were called.

She had always wondered why these dickheads get into such a state when they come to these types of low rent hotels, guess it's because they don't have to clean up after themselves. Fucking animals, its pricks like them that force her to be here on a Friday night, cleaning up their shit off the walls like a zoo keeper in an ape house.

Sally had once walked into a room to find a prostitute barley alive crawling around like a dog with worms while a guy hung from the windowsill by a tie. He had died with a clear plastic bag over his head, an orange in his mouth and his cock in his hand.

The plastic bag had been filled with poppers and he had passed out in an auto erotic asphyxiation game with the hooker.

Not knowing what to do the hooker had finished off all the drugs in the room in one go and gone quite mad.

It had taken a while for her to shake the image from her mind and they had let her have some time off. She still attended counselling and made sure that she knocked extra loud before she entered a room from then on.

It's funny, she had never even heard of people doing that sort of stuff before she had worked here. But here she was with her hand half stuffed down a toilet bowl trying to pull the remains off a teddy bear out.

Life is full of twists and turns.

There had been a guy that worked here called Mike and he had told her loads of horror stories about the types of people that frequented hotels. He had worked in the industry for years and seen it all before. He once told her about a gang of prostitutes that went around drugging footballers so they could rob them. It backfired in the end when a couple of them drugged some midget circus performers and got the sleeping drug doses wrong.

They had given the midgets enough to knock out an athletic footballer type and killed the both of them. There was a day of morning in their native home of Mexico.

Then he'd told her about some drug busts, assassination attempts, sex crimes and cheaply made pornography. Every time she saw somebody check in with a heavy bag she thought about the stories Mike had told her and thought 'what's you kink, arsehole?'

She walked down the leafy walkway towards chalet 112, the last on the list. The last occupiers had been honeymooners so she was expecting sticky sheets and the musk of a weekend of rough sex and stale champagne.

Sally fumbled with the key in the lock and let herself into the dark room. The TV was on but there was something else here.

A man stood in the middle of the room totally naked bar a pair of white cotton socks. He was balls-deep, fucking the mouth of a severed head to a backdrop of violent BDSM on the fifty inch plasma screen.

"Do come in darling, shut the door behind you. We have so much to talk about," the naked man said with a smile.

Sally felt a rush of blood to her head and her body went limp from what she was witnessing and passed out onto the boring maroon wall to wall carpet.

She noticed that the part of the carpet her face was on was quite sticky before the blackness of sleep took its hold.

## 5.

DETECTIVE INSPECTOR SIMON JENNINGS sat in the dimly lit canteen at police HQ and sipped at his fifth piss weak black coffee from the machine. The ashtray on the table had already started to overflow. He lit another cigarette and stared off into the void of deep contemplation.

But it was broken by the noisy arrival of the pigeon looking forensic guy from the crime scene fumbling for change with armfuls of paperwork and files. He spilled the contents of his woman's coin purse all over the canteen floor.

He looked around at the detective with a flustered toothy smile; his head glistened with sweat. He was still wearing that white overall and cheap suit combo that only he could wear with that level of confidence.

Detective Jennings wondered if that was the only thing he had in his wardrobe and imagined him on the dance-floor in some grotty nightclub surrounded by fat women.

He filled the drinks machine with 2p's for his 20p drink and waited for it to pour, another nervous look the detective's way this time accompanied with the wiggling of eyebrows.

*What was this guy's deal?*

Jennings just nodded and raised his cup in the man's direction.

The machine spat out his beverage with a hissing fart sound and then a series of beeps to indicate it had finished, the pigeon man had an even harder time making his way over with a boiling hot drink in a flimsy plastic cup and with all those papers. But he made it, much to the disinterest of Jennings who stared at the man in disbelief as he spread his papers over the table, spilling chocomilk into the mix for good measure.

Jennings caught a faint whiff of formaldehyde and chilled meat like in a butcher's, but what smelt like baby sick off of the pigeon man was a mystery. The cigarette smoke helped to cover most of the odour.

"Sorry for the intrusion detective but I need you to sign some release forms for some of the items you removed from the crime scene." He pushed his glasses up and dabbed at some spilt drink with a napkin. "Don't want any loose ends now do we? And it covers our arses if anything goes walkabout."

"Sure thing," Jennings drew on his cigarette, "you got a pen?"

"Of course, red or blue ink?"

"Does it matter?"

"Well I guess not, but some find writing in red ink offensive and quite rude." He sniggered and pushed his glasses up again.

"Just give me the fucking blue one." Jennings snarled.

"Yes, of course. I have a chit here somewhere for the pyramid of tits you brought out," Scampering through the papers. "That needs signing and also for the spice rack made from the dozen orbital bones, and also another for the tea towel holder made from a woman's anus."

Jennings peered at the first sheet of paper, "Sick fuck, do I sign and print?"

"Please. Then date and initial them here and here if you could, down the bottom on the dotted lines please." Handing over more pages from another file, the pigeon added, "Oh and that's for the bath filled with the various skins. You know the DNA boys are going to love that one. Just think of the overtime!"

Jennings scribbled away on page after page as the sheets just kept coming. "The faces stuck together to make some kind of wank sock, ah and the selections of arse cheeks from the spare room, dripping with jizum, had to double bag those. The sicko had filled each one like a chicken Kiev. I'll need a signature for each of those."

"Jesus, how many women did this fucker kill?"

"Ooh, hard to say but we are guessing from the limb count around sixty, give or take, maybe more. He's giving Shipman a run for his money I can tell you. Did you know he was also renting a lock up from an old man down his street?"

"What the fuck?"

"He had set up some kind of distillery in there, making moonshine out of potato skins and women's blood. There were two whole water-butts filled with blood when the boys busted the doors open."

"What the actual fuck, he's set up a factory?"

"They pulled out quite a few bottles of his home brew as well; they have it down in holding. Erm, I need you to sign this sheet for the jars of off-cuts too if you would, just once should do."

"All these bits of paper are somebody's daughter, somebody's wife, somebody's mother even."

"Some of these bits of paper are for several girls in one bag, well, bits of them anyway, oh and we are going to have a look at his old addresses. It's a long shot but there might be a body or two under a patio or something still. These guys like this start somewhere, right?"

"This fucker needs stopping."

"Well good luck with that," the pigeon man stood and started to collect all the pieces of paper and stuffed them in files, "because I have a feeling we will be seeing more of his handy work quite soon."

"Another location you think?"

"Without a doubt. A killer like this doesn't just give up, stop just like that, he's bound to get back to work soon enough." Hoisting up his glasses once again, "I wouldn't be surprised if your boys find a new site within a week, but I have to dash, got to get these papers in. And again, best of luck catching this guy." He stretched out a sweaty palm but Jennings just stared at it for a second then placed the pen into it, choosing not to shake it.

"I'll be sending down a report ASAP for you to go over once we are done cataloguing all this stuff." And with that he scurried off out of the canteen and into the darkness of a corridor.

Jennings sat back in his chair, his head still swimming from the day's events and he lit yet another cigarette. "I'm going to catch this prick and when I do I'm going to shoot him in the fucking balls."

He blew a line of smoke into the air then stubbed the cigarette on the table.

"Right in the fucking balls."

# 6.

SALLY CHOKED HERSELF awake on whatever was jammed halfway down her throat. Something solid was bobbing around in her gullet, something long being used to keep her quiet and subdued.

Her eyes blinked with tears and she was becoming aware that she was bound and upside down.

She struggled to try to free herself from her bonds but they had been tied tight, professional, a gargled scream bubbled from the strap across her mouth and then more tears. A thick mucus poured from around the thing in her throat and out through the sides of her mouth, down her face and onto the floor.

Sally was becoming aware that there was something inside her, something hard jammed inside her anus.

The more she struggled the deeper the thing inside her arse inched in. She could feel it twist further into her until she gave up and slumped from exhaustion. She belched out more of the thick saliva, it bubbled around her nose as she sighed and twitched.

She could hear movement from another room, sex noise; people were having sex in the other room, vigorous hard sex.

Sally felt a panic like nothing she had felt before and her bladder gave, a stream of urine ran down her bound body and around her neck and chin joining the puddle of mucus on the cheap laminate bathroom floor. Then the sex noise stopped and was replaced with another sound, the sound of screaming and a struggle.

The door to the bathroom suddenly burst open and a bloody naked girl flung herself through from the main room, but she stopped and stared agog for a second at the bizarre living art that was Sally trussed up, a strap on cock in her mouth, covered in her own piss with a rather large metal crucifix sticking out of her arse.

The gore covered girl screamed again.

This scream never got to finish as a claw hammer came smashing down on the top of her head and she dropped to her knees. Her eyes rolled up almost into her skull to see the damage the hammer had done.

It was Sally's turn to scream, as well as she could with big rubber dick stuffed in her neck. She saw the man that was fucking the severed head some time ago pulling the hammer from the head of the girl with a crackling slopping sound of pulped brain and fragmented skull.

"Fucking whores!" The man said kicking over the body of the girl onto the laminate floor, spilling the contents of her head out. "Take a good look you cunt." He flicked the blood from the hammer up the wall and slammed the door behind him.

Sally could not draw her eyes from the gaping hole in the girl's skull, the brain that had fallen out mixed with the now spreading blood into a large lumpy puddle around her. Her heart must have still been beating because there was the occasional pulse of blood from inside the cavity somewhere. It oozed out in a thick stew of matter and splintered bone.

Everything when red in her mind and Sally lost consciousness for a second time that day.

She wasn't in the bathroom anymore, she was somewhere very far away, and it was light and warm. The feeling of sand between her toes was so real, she could feel a cooling breeze coming from the sea and for a second she could swear that she could smell it; some strange instrument played far away and the sound of a market could be heard.

The sounds became suddenly closer, and she was sitting at a table on her own as a man in a white robe poured mint tea into a strangely painted tall glass that sparkled with colour like a stained glass window.

Faceless people passed by showing her wares and begging for money; a fire breather passed and she could feel the intense heat from the flames that flooded from his blown out cheeks. A small monkey in a waistcoat shook a cup half filled with coins at her and she threw one in; the monkey squeaked and chirped the disappeared into the crowd.

As she raised the mint tea to her freshly painted lips and she became aware of something moving in her throat, in and out, deeper and deeper and her eyes flickered from the distant dreamland of the desert market and into the conscious world.

When she realised what was going on, she wished for the desert world.

The whore killer stood over her, his thick cock sliding in and out of her mouth while he played with the metal cross stuffed in her butt. She tried to bite down hard but her mouth was being held open by some kind of vice, a gum shield covering her teeth and strapped in with cables that ran over her head.

The man stiffened and twitched in her neck and his back arched as he came deep inside her throat; her gag reflex kicked in and she vomited out past his twitching shaft and over his balls adding to the puddle of piss and blood on the floor.

He pulled out with a sucking noise and his dick was followed by more vomit as he stroked her hair looking down he smiled. The dead girl was missing from the room but for the bits of skull and brain on the floor and up the wall.

He had painted love hearts on his body with her blood and he was actually smiling; a genuine and caring smile that in other circumstances she would have fallen for.

His hand stroked her cheek tenderly and her heart pounded within her chest from the contact and he stooped to whisper in her ear.

"My love, we have all night and I have only just begun to play with you!"

# 7.

MICHAEL SAT IN his chair; a single bead of sweat ran past the bridge of his glasses and dripped off of the tip of his nose onto a mountain of paperwork. He rubbed it away with his thumb that was almost bruised from biro ink and pushed his glasses back up.

He had had enough of this damned heat and couldn't remember a time hotter.

His sweat had worked its way through his cheap shirt which now had almost transparent patches on it; the patches had spread and one of his nipples poked through. The other was covered with an extra layer of fabric from his pocket which was home to his red and blue pens.

Michael started to file away all the papers and photographs from his desk and tided up his things; a large box sat on the edge of the table and it seemed as grimy from sweat as he did.

With the box under his arm he left the building and made his way through the clammy, humidity of the night air to his shitty red Skoda in the car park.

It was a beaten thing but had never broken down. Sure it needed new everything but it was certainly a reliable old car.

He placed the box on the passenger seat and turned the key. The engine burped and spluttered then finally coughed into life.

"First time every time," smiled Michael.

The interior had the faint smell of formaldehyde and a black forest magic tree that had been there over a year. He reversed out of his spot and backed into some bushes then pulled away and out through the security gate where the guard was scanning a copy of 'Euro Butts' magazine in his little booth.

The guard broke his gaze from the grot-mag and waved Michael through the gate with a toothless smile that reminded him of a toad.

Michael's place was on the east side of town affectionately known to the locals as 'fire bin alley' due to the high amount of arson from the local kids. They would set a fire, wait for the fire brigade to arrive then start throwing stuff at them. Bricks, lumps of wood, even the occasional petrol bomb. But Michael didn't mind the area; he had lived here for years and he never had any trouble.

He had worked in the police mortuary for many years and had seen many things come and go but nothing like this, nothing to this scale.

Sure there were numerous murders during his time there; the home invasion killer, the cemetery strangler and the hypnotist rapist, but nobody with this kind of imagination, this kind of skill.

Michael was almost in awe. The mind-set of this artist must be phenomenal.

His flat was on a quiet street above a halal butcher's shop, its entrance around the back through a locked gate; a real 'you wouldn't find it if you weren't looking' kind of place, just the right kind of place for a nocturnal type like him.

The front door was at the top of a metal fire escape and the step rang as his feet stepped upon them sending flakes of chipped paint to the floor below. He jangled his keys like he had done a thousand times before in a very OCD fashion and walked in.

The place was small and cluttered with box files and storage containers intermixed with different coloured cardboard folders in various states of paper bloat.

He stepped over a pizza box and slid back the sliding doors that lead into the living room which resembled an archaic hospital museum.

There were glass jars with mutated and deformed foetuses inside, cabinets with various deformed skulls and bones, framed pictures of crime scenes and pathology photos. Several skeleton charts were used as rolling blinds over the two front room windows. It was a real treasure trove of the macabre and, for the most part, highly illegal.

The police weren't in the habit of letting one of their outsourced employees take evidence home with them. It was considered a bit of a faux pas.

He put the box down onto a writing desk in a far corner next to a print of the 'Screaming Pope' portrait by Francis Bacon and he turned on a desk lamp. He looked up at the deformed man wailing with in some unknown horror and Michael threw him a wink.

"Looking good, your Eminence."

He opened the box and pulled more files from inside which he put to one side. He then pulled a long object wrapped in black plastic out. He attacked the wrapping like an over enthusiastic child on Christmas morning, all fingers and thumbs and his tongue pocked out as he fumbled with it.

Michael ripped into it using his teeth. It grated against something hard under its wrapping. The black plastic slid away to reveal a woman's hand held together with thick copper wire that was fashioned into a twisted candle holder. He held the thing under the light to examine a little more before placing it on top of a file on the desk.

This was the sort of thing his employers would have frowned upon. Some places don't mind when you take work home but this was a different matter. This would be a centre piece for his new collection.

This was also an artefact that could land him in a whole heap of trouble.

He wasn't too worried; the pathology team had their hands full with the rest of the body part sculptures that had been removed from the crime scene. And besides, this little object wasn't even logged in. Michael had seen to that.

Michael went back into the box for another item this time unwrapped; it was a bottle of the distilled blood whiskey from the second crime scene, the old man's lock-up. Again he held it to the desk lamp and smiled to himself.

The transparent red liquid was glowing warmly under the dull bulb of the lamp. His eyes lit up at the thought of how it would taste.

"It's party time Micky boy," he broke the seal of the bottle and sniffed at the thin red liquid inside but it made him wince from the fumes of pure spirit, "better play the good host and pour a few drinks."

# 8.

BRIAN FLEXED HIS arms as he stretched in the middle of the room, his body covered head to toe in blood and shit.

Happiness had never felt like this before; he had made a breakthrough, he had found his joy.

He had only been there a couple of hours and had already claimed a honeymoon couple and a maid for materials.

The couple were more than dead and already chopped into workable parts.

Brian had no need for the male genitals and was squeezing them in his fist like a stress ball as he paced up and down. He would need one more girl to work with before he was ready to begin.

Then it hit him, the girl on the desk.

For some bizarre reason he could only recall her name as 'Juicy'; yes her, she will be the one to finish off the maid strapped up in the bathroom. He'd get her to take the maid's life as he fucked her into a coma then set about gutting the pair of them.

Brian reached for the television remote and flicked channels to a fishing show with some fat guy in waders poking at some bait hanging from a complicated looking series of lines.

He would have to find a way to lure her to the chalet.

The light blinked on in the bathroom and he stepped over the unconscious chamber maid laid out on the floor with the metal hook in her arse. Cables ran from it securing her arms behind her back and binding her feet. The big rubber dick was back in her mouth and she snorted like a pony when she breathed though her mucus filled nose.

Brian would have to get to a DIY store as soon as possible to pick up supplies, wire, cutters, and rolls of tape and lengths of copper piping. Maybe he could come up with a lure while he was out shopping. The way Brian figured it he had plenty of time.

The shower slashed into the bottom of the deep bathtub sending a fine spray over the prone maid. He twitched with the contact off the cold water and moaned but the fresh blast didn't do enough to rouse her from her sleep.

Brain washed the gore from his hair and scrubbed the dried blood from his skin before stepping into a fresh white bathrobe. He smiled down at the battered girl at his feet as the bath gurgled the last of the water down its plughole. Brian flicked off the light and closed the door behind him.

But first he would sleep, get a few hours rest. He would need his strength.

The bed was solid, the temper foam mattress absorbing his weight as he pulled over the crisp sheets and turned the volume up on the fishing show.

"When fishing a lake of this nature," the fat man in waders held up a catapult on the screen, "it's always good to pre-bait the night before, gets the fish interested in the bait balls you might use."

That's what he needed, bait.

Another smile crossed his face as he realised he had the perfect little bait ball lying unconscious on the tiled floor of his bathroom.

He would have a tidy up in the morning; put the parts of the couple into the tub before he headed out to the DIY place, just in case anyone popped their head around the door.

Brian fell asleep to the gentle sound of an acoustic guitar and the fat man talking shit about the various carp he had caught over the years. Brian still had the smile as he drifted off to the land of nod.

The guy in the bathroom isle had Steve penned onto his company name tag followed by the printed words 'always happy to help'. He was going through a list for an online customer and pulled a barrow behind him half filled with stuff to deck out a bathroom.

He hummed along to the shitty music that was being piped in via speakers overhead; he had worked there so long that it didn't bother him anymore. When he had first started it had driven him crazy but now he just filtered it out; he had become desensitised to the thrash in-store radio.

He figured that he knew every word to every Bee Gee's hit though.

Brian broke the store assistant's daydream with a small cough into his hand which made him jump a little.

"Oh, sorry I was miles away, what can I help you with today?" Steve the assistant was all fake smiles and sincerity.

Brian held out a piece of paper. "I need to get everything on this list but there doesn't seem to be anyone around except you." Brian fed him his own best fake smile in kind.

"That's typical, well this trolley can wait. Let's see if we can't get you hooked up."

Steve scurried of to fetch another cart for Brian's order while he perused the power tools and gardening equipment.

Brian's eyes darted over the heavy wood axes and garden sheers; the hedge trimmers and two foot chainsaws. Something in his pants twitched as he gazed down at a selection of scythes. He ran a finger across one of the long, curved blades and his cock thumped in his trousers.

He really shouldn't be drawing attention to him in such a manner but if people didn't give in to their urges every now and then they would just burst in an explosion of insanity. The idea made him laugh to himself.

An old woman with her husband caught sight of the man stroking the scythe blade and chuckling to himself. She hurried her husband up to stop dithering in the potted plants.

Steve popped back up with a full trolley, waving the list at face height.

"All good now. I'm just having the piping cut to length. Now are you sure you want them cut at forty five degrees?"

"Oh yes, it makes them easier to push through when they are cut to points." Brian smiled again.

Steve thought nothing of it and smiled back.

# 9.

JENNINGS SAT AT his desk chewing the end of a pencil until the wood split and the graphite crumbled into his mouth.

He spat a wad of dark grey flob into his waste paper basket and rinsed his mouth out with his coffee, his face twisted up like he had taken a bite from a black lemon, "Fucking clever."

He wiped his chin and went back to scanning the piles of photos from the crime scene; there were dozens, each with a written chit and a form with relevant info. What room the 'part' had been found was it recognisable as male or female and a brief description from the mortuary attendant, a Mr Michael Peterson, the pigeon man.

That little nerd most probably loved going through this stuff. He had heard stories about how the weird little fucker would get up to stuff at night in the morgue. Jennings had even heard that once someone found a video cassette of some dubious pornography in his locker involving a dead woman and a man in a lab coat.

It was never proven that the tape existed nor was it substantiated whether or not it was Peterson in the footage.

But he had heard things.

His eyes drifted over the photographs until they stopped on the image of a selection of arms that had been removed from one of the sculptures from the flat. Each had been bleached white and laid out in a row, connected together with metal rods and copper wire.

They had been alternated top and tail with their hands bound around cooking knives of various sizes so the blades cut into the flesh of the fingers and palms. The fucking psycho had carved the names of each of the victims into the forearms: Lucy, Jen, Steph, Alice and Claire.

The sick bastard had labelled them.

Jennings picked up the photograph and stared intently. He could feel the anger building up inside, like a pressure-head just on the red, just ready to blow but without some sort of release it would take everyone out in close proximity.

He tossed the picture on to the pile and got up, stormed out of his office and made for the gym.

The locker room was empty when he changed into his gym shorts and trainers, he wasn't the biggest of men but he kept himself trim. He was more built for running but every now and then he would come down here when it was quiet and just lay into the punch bag.

The gym was the busiest he had seen for this time of night, one guy skipping in the middle of the room and another over by the loose weights listening to music on his mp3 player.

The guy on the weights was spending more time checking himself out rather than lifting.

Jennings couldn't care less as he began to wrap his hands; he had split his knuckles and sprained his wrist on this bag before. He would just do burnout to stave off the anger; just kept punching the thing until he couldn't lift his arms anymore.

He had once wound himself up so tight with a case that he collapsed from hitting the bag for nearly an hour. Today Jennings felt he might come close to breaking that record.

An image popped into his head as he strapped the cage fighting style gloves on tight; every girl that one of the carved up arms belonged to.

He imagined a blond girl on her knees, begging for her life; then the girl turned into a brunette, then a redhead, then a different brunette.

He hadn't really noticed that he was already punching the shit out of the heavy bag.

The sweat came quickly bringing with it the burning in his arms and lungs. Image after image of the dismembered girls and the thoughts would not stop of how they suffered in their last moments.

Jennings was breathing fire and spitting lava by this point, he could feel his knuckles swelling in the tight gloves as blow after blow landed.

The two other men in the gym had stopped what they were doing and watched with the look of shock slapped over their faces. Neither of them had seen anyone hit a bag in such a way; Jennings was almost screaming with each punch thrown.

The guy that had been checking himself out while lifting waved his hands in the air and left in a hurry, quickly followed by the skipping guy who exited shaking his head.

The sweat was flying off of Jennings' arms as he crashed blow after blow into the bag, his body shaking with adrenalin and agony. With every strike another jolt of pain flashed yet more images into his mind until he felt something give.

His thumb clipped the bag awkwardly and he let out a yelp and crashed to the floor in a sweaty, shallow breathing heap.

For a moment Jennings just lay there looking up at the strip lighting, waiting for the pain in his hand to subside and his lungs to catch a few more gulps of much needed oxygen.

He rolled on to his side and leaned on his good arm to get up; still weak and shaking from the vigorous burnout of punches he got to his feet. He coughed up a huge ball of mucus as he struggled to breath and for a moment stiffened expecting to be sick. The mix of coffee and canteen food stayed in his gut.

He looked down at his damaged hand, he would have to get it seen to at some point but he didn't want to unwrap it just yet. The idea of it ballooning and bursting popped into his head; it replaced the images of all the dead girls.

Jennings regained his composure and towelled down his sweat soaked face; his hand thumped as he showered and changed from his gym cloths.

He did up his white shirt and black pencil tie, slipped white socks and black trousers on and then he threw on his grey Harrington jacket and left the changing room.

"Now let's catch this prick."

# 10.

IT WAS RAINING, only lightly but it was raining.

Michael lay on his back on the wet grass as the sun came up over the top of the trees, the fine spray in the air waking him gently from his slumber.

He wasn't really aware of anything, his body still buzzing from the blood brew he had drunk the night before. He had no idea where he was and no idea that he was naked except for his cheap white running shoes.

Michael didn't care; for the moment at least.

His eyes were stinging behind his glasses and his vision blued with a strange pink hue as if all the blood vessels in their whites had burst. There was a pain deep in his gut like he was bloated and needing the biggest shit of his life; he had half a mind just to let it go and shit himself right there on the ground.

He decided against it as the ache in his bowel shook him from his daze.

Michael sat up and looked around as he straightened his glasses; where in the hell was he? Nothing around him was familiar, he was in a park that he had never been to, surrounded by trees.

He was sitting in the middle of some kind of playing field; there was a children's play area near a public gate where a woman was talking to a police man and pointing in his direction. The woman was trying to shield the eyes of her child as she spoke to the officer.

It was then that Michael realised he was somewhat sexually aroused. Looking down he saw that he had the biggest, most raging hard on of his adult life.

His head snapped up and looked around once again, this time not in the afterglow of his trance but in panic; he had to find some way out. The trees, if he made a run for it now the policeman might not catch up with him as he was some way off.

He made the decision to bolt.

Before he really had come too he was running at full pace through the woods panting like a dog, barely able to see from the rain on his glasses.

It was at that moment that his bowel decided to give.

The sensation was not one of shame but of total release, there was something inside of him that had totally opened up and it wasn't just his quivering sphincter. For the first time in Michael's life he felt totally free, like an animal, like a wolf.

The policeman at the top of the park didn't bother to chase the streaking man; it wasn't the first time he'd had to deal with drunken student types. Besides it was more embarrassing for the guy to have to jog home in the nude.

He calmed the woman with the child down and took a statement.

It wasn't until Michael was almost home that he realized where he was. He'd crashed through some bushes that lined the park on to the main road startling a bus queue of old ladies waiting for the number seven.

He didn't stop to apologise for his shit caked nakedness.

Sneaking in through the back gate entrance to his flat he found the front door wide open and a trail of blood up the stairs. The door to his flat covered with dried blood slapped on in huge hand prints almost as if someone had tried to write something.

Cautiously he entered the small apartment, tip toeing his way into the front room to be faced with a bloodbath.

Someone had ripped a goat up from the halal butchers shop downstairs and scattered the carcass around the room.

Rib bones jutted out of lumps of meat on the floor and the walls were smeared with blood just like the front door. Then it all came flooding back.

Michael had done this, after taking the blood liquor; he had broken into the butchers and stolen the animal. He remembered peeling the skin off of the thing and wearing it as he pranced around the flat ripping into the flesh of the dead animal.

The skull; the skull was in his bedroom.

He flung the door to his bedroom open to find the skull and the hide of the animal lay out neatly over his bedclothes. He had arranged candles around the room that were still burning away. Had he performed some ritual?

He needed to get clean as the stink of his own shit mixed with the smell of dead animal blood was beginning to make him feel sick.

With his head spinning he turned on the light in the bathroom and without looking turned on the tap to the shower over the bath. He looked in the mirror to find his face smeared with blood and shit and he flipped his glasses off clumsily and dropped them into the sink.

"What have you done Michael, what have you done?"

He didn't know why but he started to laugh, and the feeling snowballed. Once again he felt alive, free, like he was the most untouchable person standing on the planet. Then something thumped in the bath tub and he craned his head to see.

Through the haze of bloodshot short-sightedness he peered past the shower curtain to see the body of a girl propped up in the bath. She was sitting with her arms around her knees; her throat had been cut from ear to ear.

She was most definitely dead.

Panicked Michael darted to and fro then scrambled in the sink for his glasses. He couldn't quite believe what he was seeing and he pulled the curtain back fully.

The girls head had flopped to one side and hit the edge of the bath, her hair matted with dried blood. The wound in her neck had gaped open like a belching frog's mouth and there were two plastic fizzy pop bottles filled with blood in the tub around her feet.

Her tongue had bloated and turned a wicked purple colour and her eyes were crossed in a comedic way; she looked like she was making a joke of the situation.

He stared at the corpse, mouth wide as if he was waiting to catch a fly.

"Oh Michael, what have you done?"

He started laughing again.

# 11.

LYDIA ON THE front desk was as bored as she had ever been in her job.

The stag party had checked out, the old couple that smelt of cabbage were in the dining room and would probably be there for the next hour or so and all the check-ins were booked to their rooms. She had literally nothing to do.

She thumbed back through an old gossip magazine that she had read three times already that week. There was an orange woman on the cover moaning about how her second marriage to some dumb-fuck cage fighter had broken down and her new book was coming out at the end of the summer.

Lydia thought the bimbo was a bit plastic and had really cheap nails but her ex-husband was a bit of alright. Lydia liked reality television and gossip columns. Deep down she had always wanted to be a celebrity; maybe she should start hanging around those trendy night clubs and bag herself a footballer, get him drunk and fuck him in a hotel lift then sell the story.

Or maybe she could sign up to one of those reality shows set on a desert island so she could show off her boobs; nothing like getting your tits out on television to get you in the national papers.

She wouldn't mind fucking someone on camera but she couldn't do porn, they only ever want to fuck girls in the arse nowadays. She had a friend that made a porno; she was fucked in the butt by two guys at the same time and got a grand in cash for her trouble.

Lydia didn't know whether she could do that; be someone's whore for a pile of cash, better to go the footballer route.

She had seen one of those sex phone-in channels on late night telly and thought "I could do that." Talk dirty on the phone while some sad act wanks himself off on the other end.

All she would have to do was lie on a bed in some studio with her tits out and gyrate.

She could defiantly do that.

Lydia rolled the magazine up and held it to her head like a phone and squeezed her breasts together and shook a little, pouting her lips like the girl she had seen on the wank channel.

"That's it baby, cum all over my…" She never got to finish her sentence as the phone rang, scaring the life out of her, and causing Lydia to send the magazine flying.

She cleared her throat and looked around the empty foyer to see if anyone had noticed the celebrity rag go flying then picked up the receiver.

"Good afternoon, front desk, how can I help you?" She was flustered and her heart had picked up a little pace from her start but she put on her best condescending receptionist voice.

"Oh, yeah, hi, I'm in chalet 112 and I've got a bit of a problem." The man on the other end of the phone had a smooth, calm voice.

Lydia remembered the man that was eyeing her cleavage when he was checking in and she thumbed at her 'juicy' necklace as he spoke.

"Right, what's the problem, sir."

"We'll its a little odd you see, it's one of your maids, she came in with some fresh towels and started to cry, something to do with her boyfriend." The man's voice remained clear and precise. "Then she freaks out and locks herself in my bathroom."

Lydia didn't quite know how to react and was almost speechless. "Oh, I see, have you tried to talk to her?"

"Yeah, but all I can get out of her is that her boyfriend is a bastard, it's all very odd."

"Very odd indeed sir, I can get one of the porters to come over and try to get the door off." Lydia really didn't know what to do.

"Wouldn't it be better if you came over, maybe a woman's voice might calm her down a bit," The voice came across as very sincere, "she is very upset."

Something in Lydia's chest sank and she felt sorry for the poor girl in the bathroom but at the same time didn't really want to get involved, but the man on the phone was right, it was better if a girl came over to help.

"Okay, I'll, get cover for the desk and be over as soon as possible, sir."

"That's great, I'll see you soon."

There was a click as the man on the other end of the phone cut the call.

Juan, one of the kitchen staff came through the foyer and Lydia waved him down.

"Can you look after the desk for me; I think Sally has had some kind of meltdown in one of the chalets." Lydia wore her best 'I like Mediterranean men' smile and stooped a little exposing the top of her ample cleavage.

"Sure Lydia," Juan being a Mediterranean man couldn't help but look at her ample cleavage, "you go help her out. It was only a matter of time I guess with the college and the pregnancy."

"Thanks, I owe you… Juan."

Juan made a fake laughing noise at Lydia's cheap attempt at a pun on his name. "I swear that's the first time I've ever heard that."

Lydia wiggled past him and out through the double door that led towards the chalets. "Love you really."

"If it wasn't for those tits she would be a horrible person." Juan picked up the celebrity magazine and sat down in the receptionist's chair.


Brian had just finished straightening the room when there was a knock at the door. He couldn't help but smile as he was greeted by the 'juicy' girl from the front desk.

"Is she still in the bathroom, sir?"

"Yeah, she's still pretty upset but I think she's unlocked the door now."

The girl crossed the room and opened the door to the bathroom. She didn't have time to scream at the sight of a pile of body parts and the crucified, anally violated twitching mess of her co-worker as Brian brought down a table lamp down onto the back of her head.

He was still smiling as he did so.

# 12.

THE NURSE WAS gentle but firm as she wrapped the last of the bandage around Jennings' hand.  She was in her late thirties with short frosted hair and little black rimmed glasses.  Cute smile, but a little band of gold on her left hand told him not to flirt too much.

"So, how did you do it?"  She looked up at him knowingly.

"Being a twat," Jennings laughed to himself.

"I had the same thing last year with my ankle in Magaluf, few drinks and I fell off a rock into the sea."

The cubicle curtain sung back and the doctor prance in holding up Jennings's x-ray to the light box on the back wall.

"Well Mr Jennings, it looks like a slight hairline fracture to your metacarpal, nothing major but we'll have to strap you up tight, no need for a cast nurse Mathews."

"Great, now I can have my lunch then," the nurse smiled back at Jennings, "Now, don't go being a twat again."  She left chuckling and shaking her head.

"So, Mr Jennings…"

"Detective."

"I beg pardon?"

"It's Detective Jennings, only the woman at the bank calls me 'Mr', it's an OCD thing."

"Right then, Detective Jennings, you'll need to rest that hand for at least a week, nothing physical for at least two."

"Great." Jennings rolled his eyes.

The doctor scribbled something on a script pad. "Take this down to the pharmacy at the front desk, a little something to help with the pain, try not to drink on them." The doctor made a sarcastic drinking motion with his hand. Why did everyone think that he was drunk when he did it?

"Much appreciated doctor." Jennings pulled his jacket on with his good hand.

"Any problems see your GP, and like the nurse said, try not to be a twat." The correction of Jennings's name was still bugging the doctor a little.

Jennings smiled to himself and made his way through to the reception area, more than pleased with himself from pissing off a doctor.

The reception was busy with a tramp propping himself up on the front desk arguing with the receptionist because his meds weren't strong enough.

"Sir, if you'll just take a seat we'll fetch the staff nurse and she can review your prescription." The receptionist was kind to the man but it was evident that she was close to kicking off; she kept a lid on it even when the tramp was being abusive.

"Listen here you skanky bitch, this shit is the same as the stuff you gave me last time and I'm telling you it doesn't fucking work." He shook the slip of paper in the woman's face; she did her best not to shove it down the homeless man's throat.

"Just take a seat or I'll have to call security, then you won't get anything will you Mr Terry?" She smiled at the man but it only seemed to enrage him further.

Jennings thought now would be a good time to whip out the badge and try to settle the stinky old menace.

"I'd do what the lady says my friend," he held up his ID wallet, "unless you want to rattle your comedown out in the cells." It caught the tramp off guard for a moment and his jaw hung open in an 'O', his tongue flopping around in his mouth looking for a few derogatory words to spit in the officer's face.

Before the tramp could react two burly security guards took him gently by the shoulders and quietly persuaded him to take his noise outside. The tramp continued to announce his disgust at his treatment at anyone within shouting distance as the security closed the doors to block out his triage of abuse.

The receptionist took Jennings's prescription out the back to give to the pharmacist while he skimmed over one of those celebrity mags with his good thumb. Some footballer on the cover, some no hoper looking for fame on a reality show on page six, celebrity spotting on page fifteen.

With every turn of the page smiling faces flashed from young starlets to the images of dead girl's lying in a pile on his desk. His thumb pulsed sending a shot of pain up his forearm as a reminder of why he was here and his stomach twisted.

Jennings tried to rub away the anguish from his eyes then a thud against the reception window snapped Jennings out of his torment and he swung round to see a huge lump of shit up the glass.

The tramp had stripped down to his dirty boots and was throwing his faeces at the security as they tried to bundle the dirty protester to the ground. The stink from the turd on the glass started to seep in through an open window and a staff nurse hurried to close it, better to be a little hot in the summer than have the reception stinking of shit.

The distraction was just what Jennings needed to keep his mind off of all the dead girls and he laughed at himself.

The pharmacist handed a small paper bag over the back counter to the receptionist and she handed it over to the broken-handed policeman.

"That's two in the morning and two in the afternoon after eating, top up with one in the evening if pain persists." She smiled down at Jennings. "How would you like to pay?"

"I don't have to fucking pay for these," He waved the packed in the air. "I'm a police officer."

"And this is a pharmacy not a fucking charity so it's £7.60 or you can run your thumb under a fucking cold tap and fuck off while you're doing it." The receptionist had clearly had enough for one day and wasn't budging on the price.

"This fucking country," Jennings mused and pulled a ten note free from his wallet and slapped it on the counter. "Keep the change love, get yourself a new attitude."

"Thank you, sir, try not to injure yourself WANKING AGAIN!" She shouted it loud enough for everyone in the waiting in the reception area to hear... bitch.

Jennings chuckled to himself as he left the reception and out into the courtyard where the tramp was being bundled into the back of an ambulance. The two security guys stood back as the ambulance men struggled to get the vagrant strapped in.

His phone started to play some television theme tune in his jacket pocket as Jennings negotiated his way through the floor-maze of tramps clothes and lumps of shit.

"Simon?" It was Jennings's partner Biloff, his strange Hungarian accent sounding excited. "We have an ID on that sick fucker's number plate. He was spotted outside some DIY place about seventy five miles away. Do you want me to pick you up?"

"Yeah, I'm over at accident and emergency, I'll explain on the way." A broad smile spread across his face as he dropped his phone back into his jacket pocket. "We've got you now, fuck head!"

# 13.

**THE DISMEMBERED PARTS** of the girl hung from the shower curtain rail on coat-hangers used as makeshift hooks. The pieces were dripping into the bath below.

He was determined to catch every last drop of the glorious stuff. The deep red against the cold white of the tub made his dick twitch.

Michael sat caked in dried blood on his toilet staring into the eyes of the girl he found there only an hour or so ago. She looked back at him with a blank expression, the muscles in her face somewhat drooped as if she had suffered a stroke.

He smiled at her. She did not respond.

Michael needed to get into the evidence room of the police station to get to some of the note books from the lock up crime scene. There would be the recipe for the blood cocktail that he had ingested that caused him to go on the rampage the night before in there somewhere.

He could still feel the strange brew's effects shaking their way out of his pores.

For the moment he had found every plastic bottle and sealable jar around his flat to collect the blood so he could store it in his fridge until he could get his hands on the notes.

Then it dawned on him, he had an artefact from the first crime scene; he could make up some bullshit about it getting mixed up with something else or some hiccup with paperwork and he had to take it down to be logged. He had done it before. If it wasn't for the lies he wouldn't have gained such an impressive collection of macabre objects.

He washed in the sink with a bar of soap and a face flannel then towelled himself down. Everything that had come into contact with his skin was now a grisly shade of pink. Michael dressed in the other room in his trademark cheap suit, glasses and well-worn jacket. Then he wrapped the female hand candelabra he had stolen in newspaper and stuffed it into his coat.

Michael noticed there was just a little of the blood-spirit left in the bottle. He sank the last of it in one glug and waited for the burning to roll down his throat and into his belly. Almost immediately he felt the effect, his skin rippled with tiny pin pricks of electricity and the hair on the back of his neck stood on end.

Once again Michael felt alive.

The evening was quiet down his street. The usual gang of kids outside the off licence were being loud but he wasn't in the mood to converse.

"Yes blud, it's that weirdo from the butchers, what you saying?" One of the youths threw an empty energy drink can at

Michael's car. It bounced off the driver's side window and clattered to the floor.

Usually he would let it go. He didn't want to upset the locals and tried his best to keep under the radar but with the blood brew surging around his veins something was different.

He was different.

"I'll tell you what I'm fucking saying." The spirit in him was talking now as he rounded the car to pick up the can. "I'm sick of you lot out here every night doing drugs and harassing good people."

The group of youths bunched up and stepped forward, arms wide and hooting like howler monkeys.

"The fuck you say blud, the fuck you say?" The youths were jumping all over each other to get to Michael. He rushed forward to meet them.

"I'll tell you the fuck I just said you uneducated fuckwits, you!" He grabbed the lead youth by the neck and started to slam the can into his face. The can started to rip open with the force of the blows slashing into the soft skin of the mouthy teen.

Teeth and blood started to fly from the kid's mouth as the crushed can struck again and again, Michael's fist gaining speed with every punch.

The rest of the gang rained blows down on Michael but nothing seemed to hurt; kicks and punched just seemed to bounce off of him without leaving so much as a sting.

With the face of the kid suitably stowed in Michael dropped the can and turned his attention to the rest of the gang. His fists began to fly with deadly accuracy; it was almost like he had removed himself away from time and reality when he moved. Everything around him had slowed somewhat and he could see punches coming well before they had been thrown; just enough time for him to duck, cover or counter.

The gang went flying, each holding part of their face or head with blood pouring from each savage blow that Michael landed.

It was a good minute before Michael realised every one of them was flat out on the ground either moaning from their injuries or asleep.

Michael snorted his own blood from his nose and dusted himself down; looking up he noticed the old Indian man that owned the shop giving him the thumbs up. A smile jumped on to Michael's face, he had gone from local weirdo to man of the people in a matter of moments.

He started his car and headed towards the police station; in all the excitement he hadn't noticed that his cock had got hard or that he was driving faster than he had ever driven before.

He was buzzing, he was alive.

But his new found glory was nothing in comparison to his goal, his plan; the idea of stilling his own blood spirit and living with the psychotic power that it would bring charged him. He now was more determined than he had ever been.

But he had no idea what he was doing.

All he had to do was break into a secured fortress filled with armed guards all looking to tag some deranged serial killer and take papers that were part of an ongoing national investigation.

He was playing it by ear but with how he was feeling nothing would stop him.

He was indestructible.

# 14.

BRIAN HAD THE room all sorted out.

The two girls that he had left alive were bound and laid out in the centre of the room; he had also barricaded the glass patio doors at the back of the chalet with the queen sized bed. This served two purposes, one to keep out unwanted visitors and second it served as a cheap soundproofing for what he had in mind for his girls.

The girls wriggled in the middle of the carpet like gigantic maggots, the bleach he had scrubbed them down with already working its magic on their living skin.

Juicy, the receptionist, had already got it in her eyes and they had started to blister and puss like the eyes of a cooked fish while the cleaner girl's hair had started to wither and turn a pale blond.

He stood over them rubbing his hands together. For a brief moment he felt excitement well up in him, it was almost like the anticipation of the first Christmas he could remember as a child.

Grinning from ear to ear he lay down with the girls, rolling them towards his naked body. They were the bread with him as the cheese in the middle. Brian cradled them in his arms for a while listening to their sobs from under the duct tape, he wiped away the tears from their cheeks and hushed them quiet as he rocked the tortured women.

He lay his head down into Juicy's shoulder while cupping Cleaner's breast. Brian nuzzled her neck breathing in her smell, the scent of her skin, her perfume and the shampoo in her hair, although all of it was smothered with the stink of bleach. But he could smell the scents under the bleach, over the overpowering odour of chlorine.

The two girls looked into each other's eyes in the hope to find some solace but all they saw was terror and their own impending doom. This only brought on more tears as the psychotic man between them pulled the two slices of bread tight to his cheese-body.

He had become noticeably aroused.

"You see I love you, girls." He rolled over to face Sally. "I have such great place for you, the both of you." He flopped back on to his back and stroked Lydia's slowly whitening hair. "You are going to be immortalised, glorified for the entire world to see. Together you will be a beautiful opera and I will be your conductor."

Brian jumped to his feet, his raging hard on jutting out from his groin life a flagpole. He leant over and grabbed the cleaner girl's ankles and with a stern twist flipped her on to her belly, her hands were tapped together underneath her body and she shook with fright as he spread her arse cheeks to assess the damage he had done earlier.

"You girls really don't know how lucky you are, you are going to be talked about from here to Bombay." The laugh he let out made the bound girls shudder. "We together will be the centre piece of the greatest art installation the universe has ever seen."

Sally whimpered under her gag and as the tears streamed down her face, she tried her best to shut herself off from the ordeal, to find a happy place that she could go to and close out the horror but it hadn't worked. The only respite she had was when she was unconscious.

She was hoping the last time she came to that this had all been some dream, a landscape she had made for herself after being sent into a coma from an accident. She would wake and see her family around her, her infant daughter, her mother and her friends.

Alas, she was still here. Once again she felt the dry wind of some far-away desert caress her face and longed to be back at the market bazaar. She wondered if that was where people went when they died.

The sensation was replaced soon enough by the stifled screams of the girl next to her being turned over and admired by the man with the hard on.

Lydia tried with all her might to kick the man away but she was bound far too tightly to get any real leverage and she floundered in panic in the middle of the floor. The man knelt over her, kneading at her buttocks and probing with his fingers; he was going to enjoy her.

Brian buried his face into her arse and she screamed behind the tape; he had taken the dildo gag from the throat of the cleaner girl and was looking to shove it somewhere. He wanted to enjoy the girl before he fixed the head gear to her.

He had made a long spear from the angle cut copper piping and rigged it with leather strapping that would slip over Juicy's head; it looked very much like an old Gatling gun from one of those westerns he had seen as a child. His mind wandered for a second and imagined Juicy bent double as Brian turned the hand crank sticking out from her ribs, the rig on her head spinning and spitting bullets at a horde of marauding Mexican bandits.

CHUKA, CHUCKA, CHUCKA!

The gun coughed out that childish toy gun sound as one by one the Mexicans fell, ripped into pieces from the barrage of fire from the grotesque human machine weapon.

CHUCKA, CHUCKA, CHUCKA!

He shook the thought clear and smiled as he lifted the apparatus he was going to war. Brian had built one for himself that would fit to his dick. He was going to fuck Juicy while she face fucked the cleaner.

He was going to ride the pair of them into the next world then arrange them in such a way that he would be remembered forever, a crowning achievement, the cherry on the cake. But what would draw the world attention to him, to this place?

He would have to make a grand gesture, a last stand that would leave a scar on this part of the world forever, a mark that you could see from the far reaches of the universe. He would have to build a spire to the macabre; a tower that would change the way man viewed man.

It was at that moment that Brian decided to kill every last person in the hotel.

# 15.

THE BLACK MERCEDES pulled into the bus lane outside the hospital to the general disgust of the people waiting for the Fast-track B; the driver gave the finger to an old woman that was trying to wave the car away.

DI Jennings cut through the crowd holding aloft his badge and rounded to the driver's side and tapped the credentials against the window. The driver rolled down the smoked glass to reveal a man in a baseball cap with a thick black goatee beard.

"What's the problem, officer?" The driver's accent was eastern European and deep.

"You know you can't park here, sir."

"I'm just picking someone up, officer, just a couple of minutes."

"Tell him to fuck off." The old lady that had been given the bird grunted and shook her fist angrily at the driver.

"Please calm down, madam," Jennings waved away the old lady's comments then turned his attention back to the driver. "But she does have a point, why don't you fuck off, sir?"

"Because I'm waiting for your mother to swing by to suck my cock," the driver calmly replied.

There was a stunned silence at the bus stop. Every single face in the queue was agog at the driver's audacity.

The officer went around to the passenger side of the car and opened the door. "You have left me no choice, sir," Jennings jumped into the passenger seat and slammed the door shut, "take me to Burger Shed you fat Hungarian bastard."

The Mercedes roared off from the bus stop wheels spinning off into the main road leaving the people looking puzzled to what they had just witnessed.

"You broke your fucking hand on a punch bag?" Biloff was laughing so hard he had to spit the mouthful of cheeseburger into the drive-thru bag.

"Yeah, ha-ha, get it off your chest." Jennings looked out of his window to try to hide his mild embarrassment, dipping his fries into the little plastic pot of barbecue sauce.

"I thought you would have learnt your lesson from last time." Biloff's laugh was making the windows rattle.

"Listen, I had a bad day and I wanted to take it out on something, just caught the bag wrong, that's all."

The burly Hungarian took another giant bite of his burger then spoke through the food. "You shouldn't let it get to you like that, man." He wiped the ketchup from his chin. "You're going to have to take a holiday after this case, get away from it all. Otherwise, you'll end up burning out if you don't."

"Fuck it, you haven't seen the photos. This fucker needs bringing down and fast."

"You're not wrong, brother." Biloff took a slug from his vat of 7up. "There was an ID on the car up north, a DIY place, they sent up a few plain clothes to ask around, apparently he did a little shopping then fucked off with no trace."

"No trace, no lead."

"You say that but there's CCTV all over those industrial estates, probably get a positive ID and an idea which way he headed."

"Fuck, that prick could be halfway across the country by now." Jennings paused from dipping his fries, "But saying that, if he's shopping for stuff he's got to have a nest somewhere nearby. This kind of high functioning killer is going to want to get to work as soon as possible, especially now that the clock is ticking."

"He'll need somewhere out of the way, somewhere quiet. For all we know he could have lock-ups all over the country." He admired the burger for a second and picked his spot before filling his mouth.

Jennings was also stuffing his face. "Not our guy. If this type knows we're coming he's going to want to show us something. Like one last gesture to wave in our face before we catch him." He glanced at his partner, "And we will catch him."

There was stillness in the car for a moment as both men realised that Jennings was right, this killer wouldn't stop. He wouldn't go to ground not now that he was out in the open. He couldn't. The man they were chasing was a craftsman, an artist and now he would want everyone to see his work. He would not be able to help himself.

Biloff's mobile phone rang and vibrated across the dashboard making the two men flinch slightly as its noise invaded their silence.

They looked at each other for what seemed like an hour before Biloff picked up the handset and answered, "Biloff."

Jennings sat finishing his fries, he could just hear the voice on the other end, it was frantic and Biloff looked a little worried as he finished the call.

"No problem, we're on our way."

"What?"

"They got a positive ID on our man."

"And?"

"We might have a lead after all."

"What lead?"

"Two hotel workers, both female haven't made it home. They just vanished apparently; the place is quite close to where this prick was sighted."

Another moment of stillness and this time it was one that neither of the men welcomed. Both wanted it to be a coincidence but they both knew it was their man.

"Shit." Jennings was the first to break the silence. "So where's the hotel?"

"About five miles from the DIY place."

"Better start there then."

"Better finish my burger first."

"You better had."

Before Biloff picked up the last of his meal he looked at his partner. "I have a bad feeling about this, brother."

Jennings said nothing and returned to looking out of the window, Biloff went back to his food and crunched at a hanging piece of pickle.

The pain in Jennings thumb came back for a second, just to let him know it was still there and wanting a top up of the prescribed pain killers. Jennings obliged and washed down two of the tiny pills with a swig of his fizzy orange drink, the last of the sickly liquid slurped up the straw.

While Biloff wedged the last corner of his burger into his mouth Jennings recalled the moment he walked into the basement flat dressed in his forensic gear. He remembered the heat in the room and the smell of decay.

He was not looking forward to walking into another of this sick freak's work rooms.

As the car started he threw a though the way of the two missing hotel workers and hoped they had just gone out together. He wanted them to be found drunk in some kebab shop singing and throwing salad around alive and well at two in the morning.

Maybe they had run away together in some lesbian love pact and were heading for Paris or Rome or Barcelona, happy and free in their new life.

He knew that that was wishful thinking.

# 16.

MICHAEL WAS HAVING trouble with his key-card. Swipe after swipe the red light flashed up with an annoying 'BEEP' and it was making him angry. He could actually hear the blood in his temples throb. He was still fired up from the last of the wicked red spirit and it was all he could do to not smash the reader.

A voice crackled over the card reader's intercom. "Do you need any help there, mate?"

Michael was on the verge of screaming at the man on the intercom but thought against it. He was so close he didn't want to blow it now.

"Yes, hello there, I seem to be having trouble with my key card, my name is…"

The crackly voice cut him off. "I know who you are, mate, what's the problem with the card?"

Michael held it up near to the tiny camera in the intercom and inspected it, there was a crack running across the magnetic strip. It must have been damaged in the fracas outside the off licence.

"It seems to be a little damaged; I must have sat on it or something." His heart was pounding in his chest and his teeth started to grind, the smile for the camera was starting to frustrate.

"I suppose you want to come in then?" By now Michael had worked out that the security guards were taking the piss out of him.

"I wouldn't mind. I have something for the evidence room that we've had in the lab for a while." Michael's jaw and neck locked up slightly from fear that they would work out that he had driven in through the main gate.

"No worries, just ask nicely and we'll let you in."

"I beg your pardon?"

"Ask... nicely." The security guard's voice condescending like he was talking to a child. Michael had to maintain, he couldn't lose it now.

Michael exhaled deeply. "Okay, can I please enter the building so I can put this human hand into evidence, pretty please with sugar on top?" He pulled the hand candle holder from his coat and freed it from the newspaper to show the camera.

"Fucking hell!" the voice on the intercom was now in shock and it was followed by the familiar 'BUZZ' from the door's magnetic lock.

"Thank you," Michael pulled the door open, "you fucking prick!"

The station was quiet and there was no one in the break room as Michael negotiated his way down to evidence. In fact there wasn't anyone anywhere; he didn't see a sole officer until he got down the holding area. There a single desk sergeant sat reading the paper at the booking in desk while a Scottish drunk screamed at him through the observation hatch.

Michael was half tempted to get his attention and ask where everyone was but the fewer people knew he was here the better and he slipped through the side door. The desk sergeant didn't even look up from the sports section when he heard the door close at the other end of the corridor.

This was all too easy and it made Michael nervous, he was still shaking from the effects of the blood spirit but knew he would have been shaking with fear if he wasn't 'high'.

His cheap shirt was soaked with sweat, his forehead burned with fever. Michael's eyes darted from door to door expecting a heavily armed security guard to come charging at him, but they didn't come, nobody came.

Smooth sailing all the way down to the evidence room.

Big Del was on the evidence desk, a result as he had always found Michael a bit of an oddity and as good as harmless. Big Del had no idea that Michael had walked out on countless occasions with this and that under his dirty old rain coat.

The big man's bald head glistened with sweat under the artificial strip lighting and he too was thumbing through the sports section of the day's paper.

"And a hello to you Del." Michael tried to act as casual as possible.

"Ah, hello back there Mike. So what brings you down to the depths today?" Big Del's smile was as broad as his shoulders.

"Just bringing some stuff from that twisted crime scene the other night, left overs."

Del chuckled. "You path-lab boys and your sense of humour, fill your boots." His shovel of a hand slipped under the desk and pressed the button to 'buzz' Michael into the evidence cage.

Michael found a large evidence bag and slipped the hand into it, logging the artefact into the book on the desk. He scanned down the page and found the note books he wanted, lot 132d, bingo.

"Grisly stuff, so where is everyone today." Michael pushed his glasses up his nose with the log book pen.

"All called out, apparently they have a lead on the nutter that brings you down here."

"Really," Michael's ears pricked up, "where are they headed exactly?"

"Don't really know, I was in the break room then there was a mad rush and everyone fucked off. I guess they must have caught up with the fucker."

Michael slinked to the back of the room and located the note books. "Really, sounds all high risk and whatnot."

"Yeah, looks like we might have our work cut out over the next week I reckon." Big Dell flipped the paper open to page three and stared down at the young blond in a swimming pool beaming up from the page with her tits hanging out. "Still, keeps us all in overtime."

"You're not wrong Del." He slid the books into his coat and left the cage. "Well I guess I'll see you in a day or two."

"Yep, you go safe now." Michael was already gone by the time Del had finished the sentence.

He raced out of the station and to the safety of his car. His body had started to ache from the withdrawals of the blood spirit. He was going to have to get to work soon.

He reached over to his glove box and took out his police band scanner, turned it on and it spat static at him inter-cut with the occasional burst of frenetic alphabet and commands from officers on patrol.

He would have to keep a sharp ear to the scanner while he went over the note books. It's going to be a long night.

# 17.

KNOCK, KNOCK, KNOCK.

The businessman in room 16 woke up with a start and didn't know whether the knock at the door was part of a stress dream. He rubbed the sleep from his eyes and looked around to get his bearings, another shit hotel and another shit toilet roll seminar.

KNOCK, KNOCK, KNOCK.

It wasn't a dream and he wearily slipped out of the deluxe queen sized bed and into the tatty complimentary slippers and bathrobe. He staggered over to the door still reeking of hotel restaurant curry and overpriced beer.

He was greeted by a tall man in typical hotel waistcoat and 'can I help you' smile stood in the hallway.

"Sorry to disturb you, sir." The man at the door held up his hands like he was praying. "But the silent alarm seems to have tripped in your bathroom. I've just come to check it out."

"Silent alarm?" he asked and before the tenant knew what was going on the hotel employee was in the room and heading towards the bathroom.

"Yes, it happens all the time, new system you see, nine times out of ten it's just someone smoking but as I say it's a new system and it has a few gremlins."

"Oh, well I don't smoke."

"Not saying you do sir, not saying you do, you see, there that little red light is blinking, probably faulty." The employee pointed to a plastic dome on the bathroom celling. The businessman peered at the thing but didn't see any red light.

"I don't see any…"

As the man turned the employee's forehead crashed into his nose, sending him back hard against the sink. The solid corner succeeded in snapping one of his lower ribs. The man flopped to the floor coughing out blood and holding his crumpled nose, gushing red over his trembling hands.

The employee's foot came down hard against the man's head that was wedged against the wall at an awkward angle. The hard sole of his high polished shoe finding temple again and again until the rigidity of the man's skull gave and the side of his head caved in.

Brian stood over the dying man in triumph and gave him one last stamp in the face to finish the job good and proper.

He cleaned himself up over the body of the still twitching business man and searched the room for something he could use to clean up the next room. Brian found a tennis racquet in a sports bag and a childish grin crossed his face.

He took out a scrap of paper with the names and room numbers of all the guests left, only another twelve rooms to get through. Next up, room 19; the honeymoon couple.

KNOCK, KNOCK, KNOCK.

"Rooooooooom service!"

As soon as the door opened the woman on the other side was greeted with a backhand that would have won match-point at Wimbledon. With a stunning 'twang' the volley sent the woman flying back into the room and over the bed where her new husband was laying, watching television.

The man in the bed shot up only to be sent the way of his wife with a swipe from the racquet swung at his jaw like an axe. The man's mandible bone shattered at the joint sending him unconscious before he hit the ground.

Brian then turned his attention to the wife who was struggling to get to her feet, the racquet now turned around with the handle poised to be rammed into something.

KNOCK, KNOCK, KNOCK.

Brain had given up with the pleasantries; this was now an all-out room invasion.

The spike of the umbrella slammed into the soft pulp of the builder from Hartlepool's right eye, through the brain, jamming on the back wall of his skull.

Brian wrestled the man back into the room and shoved down hard on the brolly until it popped out the back of the man's head.

KNOCK, KNOCK, KNOCK.

The prostitute in room 27 didn't even have time to get off her knees when her punter crashed into her with a claw hammer stuck in the top of his head.

Before she could scream the door was slammed shut and Brian's hand was down her throat looking to pull something back up.

He balled it into a fist and she felt all the rings of cartilage in her windpipe burst as he ripped it back out through the gaping hole.

KNOCK, KNOCK, KNOCK.

Room 31; kick in the bollocks to another businessman followed by an ice bucket to the face, again and again and again.

KNOCK, KNOCK, KNOCK.

The woman from Wales who was visiting her sick grandmother was greeted with a plastic bag over the head and struggle-fucked to death on the floor of room 40.

KNOCK, KNOCK, KNOCK.

Room 46, knife in the groin, male on business from Rochdale.

KNOCK, KNOCK, KNOCK.

Room 49, battered with a heavy glass ashtray, homosexual couple on a dirty weekend.

KNOCK, KNOCK, KNOCK.

Room 54, strangled and broken neck with bare hands, female traveling from Aberdeen to London.

KNOCK, KNOCK, KNOCK!

KNOCK, KNOCK, KNOCK!

KNOCK, KNOCK, KNOCK!

Brian rolled the last of the corpses off of the hostess trolley and on to the polished wooden floor of the dancehall. The pile was filled with the battered bodies of staff and guests alike, an impressive collection of materials.

He strolled out whistling a jaunty tune to return the trolley to the kitchen and collect a few knives for the job in hand.

Then he checked the front doors were still locked and chained all the fire doors and staff entrances, went room to room locking all the windows and room doors. The place was totally locked down.

Brian had painstakingly printed out a sign for the front door before he started to clean house and stuck it to the reception window.

It read –

*Due to a committee decision the hotel will be shut indefinitely. All staff will be asked to call in on Monday to be handed redundancies. All guests will be refunded. We are sorry for any inconvenience caused.*

That should keep any prying eyes away for the night.

Brian was happy, for now he could begin his greatest creation without any interruptions. He was almost bouncing as he entered the dance hall. Now it was a case of stripping all the bodies and bleaching them before he could sculpt them into the greatest art installation ever conceived.

He would be remembered for all time.

# 18.

JENNINGS AND BILOFF pulled into the car park of a rundown motorway hotel and parked up as close to the main entrance as they could. The pair looked at the grim throwback of a building and got out.

"What a fucking shithole." Biloff was unimpressed with the location.

"I second that, looks like someone took a shit in America and shipped it over here in the seventies." Jennings squeezed his broken thumb under the bandaging; the numb pain was somehow reassuring.

Biloff had jogged up to the front doors; finding them to be locked he read the notice in the window shaking his head.

"What's up Biloff?"

"The place is shut down, something about a committee." Biloff went to the back of the car and popped the boot. "This isn't good, if the place is shut down and there are no guests whose are all the fucking cars."

Jennings looked around at the partially full car park and his heart sank. His partner had a rather grave point; there were a hell of a lot of cars for a place that was out of business.

The Hungarian pulled a black holdall out and dumped it on the roof; unzipped it and pulled out a semi-auto pistol and handed it to Jennings. He pulled out another for himself followed by a hunting knife that he clipped to his belt.

"You want a couple of clips with that, Simon?" Biloff waved two filled 9mm magazines at his partner.

"Fucking right I do, I want to make sure this prick is all the way dead."

"There will be no coming back from where we will send him." Biloff pulled on a pair of leather gloves. "We'll have to phone this in, get heavy duty down here."

"Better had, but I still want to be in there as soon as possible, if this fucker is in there where are all the guests?" Jennings shook his head as he checked his weapon. "I think we are in for a long night my brother."

"I hope not, Bitchin' Kitchen is on tonight." Jennings threw his partner a raised eyebrow, Biloff just grinned back at him. "What, I have a thing for Nadia G."

Even with the grim prospect of entering the hotel Jennings still managed a smile as his partner phoned through the situation to the operations officer.

The pair rounded the main entrance into a communal garden; it was void of guests and quiet as the grave. Every window and a set of patio doors had their curtains closed. The men tried to sneak a peek through any cracks but to no avail.

"We're going to have to pop a window, brother." Biloff was already to smash the glass of the patio doors with the butt of his pistol.

"Hold up big guy, we might want to find a quieter way in." Jennings pointed towards the beer cellar hatch by the side of the building.

The pair stalked over to the entrance with Biloff ready to open the hatch. Jennings held up his weapon to cover his partner. Biloff tugged at the corner of the twin door hatch and was surprised that it moved.

"Health and safety would have a field day here." He looked at his partner. "Steady when I open this, don't want to shoot some waiter."

Jennings nodded in agreement and to signify that he was ready; Biloff threw the door open and Jennings stiffened up but there was nothing but a dusty beer cellar.

"You want to go first, brother?" Biloff signalled with his eyes towards the hatch.

"After you, I'm injured remember." Jennings held out his bandaged hand and smirked.

"You always have an excuse."

Biloff descended into the gloom of the cellar with his pistol down by his side; if he was honest he would rather be at his desk processing paper work right about now. He scouted around the cold, dank room to find nothing but spiders, barrels and boxes of various bottles.

"It's clear down here."

Jennings was already at the bottom of the chute and crossing the room to meet his partner.

The cellar door was open and a long corridor run under the entire hotel. At the far end was another room similar to the cellar with a staircase that must have led to the bar area. The walls of the room lined with shelving, home to bottle upon bottle of hard liquor. The room smelt of stale alcohol and cigarette smoke.

Jennings held his breath for a moment; it felt as if he was at the gates of hell. The images of dead girls still flicking through his mind and a pressure began to build in the front of his skull. The thump of blood in his hand sent another pulse of pain up through his arm letting him know that he was still alive, still in the real world.

Biloff checked the bottom of the stair; his pistol poised as he put a finger to his lips to hush his partner then started the assent into the hotel bar.

Jennings watched the large frame of his partner climb the stairs and round the corner, Biloff waved him up and disappeared into the bar. Jennings took a deep breath and followed.

The bar was empty and dark; every table untouched. Shafts of dull light poured into the still room through small cracks in the curtains reflecting off of the glasses stacked above the bar filling the room with an eerie glow.

Across the room flashing disco lights threw dashes of colour onto the round windows of a set of double doors. Music thumped inside the room; above the doors read a sign, 'Dance Hall'.

The two men spread out and crossed the room, both holding their weapons out in front of them pointing directly at the doors to the dance hall.

Biloff got to the doors first and pressed himself up against the wall next to them. Jennings hung back a little anticipating his partners boot to the door and lock his shooting stance ready for whatever was waiting behind the doors.

He felt the need to just rush the dance floor and put as many bullets into whoever was in there; there was a chance it was just a party but he knew deep down that it wasn't the case.

Jennings took another deep breath and nodded to his partner who turned and slammed his foot into the door almost sending it off its hinges as the pair burst into the room.

# 19.

HE TRAWLED THROUGH the note book and scribbled on scrapes of paper. Stacks of photos and files strewn all over the floor of the small flat.

The wall over the fireplace was now an evidence board covered with post-its and images, notes and newspaper clippings; lines of red string criss-crossed a large map of the town, each line nail in with tiny pins.

Michael was sweating over his work, constantly pushing back his glasses with the end of his pencil as they slid down the bridge of his nose from all the frantic head turning.

It was like his skin was on fire. He was burning up, covered with sweat and couldn't concentrate for more than a second on any one thing. His hands were shaking and he had a terrible thirst unlike anything he had experienced before.

He was coming down, hard.

The blood spirit had all gone and Michael was now stuck with several bottles of harvested gore and a collection of body parts from the body of a woman he had come home to. Michael still had no idea who she was or where she had come from. It did not concern him, what was done was done. He had bigger fish to fry before his withdrawal sent him mad.

The body parts had started to turn from the summer heat and for once he was glad that he lived above a butchers shop. The stink of the halal goat meat downstairs was doing a bang up job of covering the faint smell of corpse, emanating from his bathroom.

All this was sound-tracked by the police scanner that crackled and popped. And it joined occasionally with voices that belched code and directions. Somewhere out there were women at the control centres logging every number and street name and filling incident reports. They communicated with the officers on the ground with codes of their own, information and instructions on protocol.

Michael listed intently, as much as his running mind set could allow until finally he heard it, the call he was waiting for.

It started with nothing more than the familiar crackle of static, then a dead spot followed by a sharp beep.

"6 5 opps to control."

"Go ahead 6 5."

"Got a call from Jennings and Biloff concerning their case requesting armed back up ASAP, over."

"No problem, send over details and I'll cover the request, over."

"Will do control. Let's hope they have good news, over."

Michael's heart pounded as the details came through. He was having no joy with the notebooks. Maybe if he met the man face to face he could find out his secrets, get the recipe straight from the horse's mouth.

He stood, his body stripped down to his pants and he went into a headless chicken like panic.

Michael darted to and fro looking for clothes and keys and shoes and wallet; he had to move quickly before the man that held the key to his future was shot to shit by a SWAT team.

In the frenzy he buttoned his shirt askew to the holes, slipped into odd socks, put his shoes on the wrong feet... twice and nearly strangled himself with his own tie. But he managed to settle himself for a moment to find his car keys.

Before he knew it he was scooping up the bottles of blood from his fridge and bagging up the mystery dead woman's head in his coat.    Perhaps he could suggest to the killer some sort of offering, some sort of gift in trade for the secret of the blood spirit.

Even through the hazy tail end of his blood-buzz he had never been more focused.  He knew what he needed, Mikey needed his sugar.

His skin itched as he hit the motor way.  The crackling scanner was next to him on the passenger seat, along with the head and the bottles of blood.

The air con in his clapped out old car was beyond broken and the sweat poured from his skin as he shook out the last of his blood fix.  He made the decision to strip off as he drove, but he would have to speed up overtaking high sitting trucks, but he was long past giving a fiddler's flying fuck.

So here he was, speeding up the motorway towards a hotel that was by now crawling with armed police.  Michael was wearing nothing but a tie and glasses, and progressing through the City with the remains of an unknown woman rolling around next to him.

He turned to look out the window.  As he passed a car filled with young girls, they pointed and laughed at the skinny naked man grinding his teeth, gripping the steering wheel like his life depended on it.

He bared his teeth at the car.  They laughed harder but they were a second later silenced as Michael spewed up the glass of his window and then he drew a penis in the thick vomit with his finger. He swerved his heap of a vehicle across the lane, throwing it into the side of the stunned girl's car and sent them careering off of the road and into the crash barrier.

The car crumpled and rolled over the barrier coming to a stop on its coverable roof that was now all the way caved in.

"I hope you're all dead you pack of screeching cunts."

Part of Michael wanted to go back and play with them for a while, setting up the dead or dying women in sexual positions for the authorities to find. The idea took the edge off of his comedown for a moment, something about the ideas of violence and perversity helped him with the pain.

The stink of vomit turned Michael's stomach and he threw up again into his own lap but he didn't look away from the road like it was the most natural thing in the world. The warmth of the sick tickled his balls and his dick started to thicken from the sensation. This also helped with the pain and he decided to masturbate in his puke as he zipped between cars.

He was half tempted to stick his dick in the open neck hole of the severed head but didn't want to stop or crash his car to untangle it from his knotted up coat.

He would just have to make do with jerking it up the motorway as Michael sat in a wide, spreading pool of his own barf.

# 20.

AFTER STRIPPING ALL the wire from one of the conference rooms and killing the telephone lines he had spent the rest of his time chopping up corpses and bleaching them in a bucket.

Like an expert tailor he used the copper wire stitching. He treaded the parts together from a needle he had fashioned from a splinter of the copper piping. It slipped through the skin and flesh of the dead with ease, the wire squeaked on contact of bleached skin as it was dragged through and pulled tight.

He sat in the middle of the dance floor; his cock raging hard, piecing together his finest work. Every now and then he let out a little squirt of spunk from the excitement.

Brian had weaved the severed limbs together to create chicken-wire-like dome in the middle of the dance hall, held up with the dead people's belts, shoelaces and ripped up knotted bed sheets.

The two girls that he had kept alive were strapped into a frame that he had made from old furniture and more of the copper wire.

Juicy's head hung down with the weight of the spear-like headgear; she was knelt behind the cleaner girl whose head was taped to the ground, her arse stuck up in the air ready for the insertion of the copper pipe lance.

Brian was wearing his own homemade spear. It bobbed around jutting out from his hips as he hopped around the limb-cage checking everything was in place. He had cut a vagina out from one of the corpses and affixed it inside the makeshift strap-on; he was to gain a little stimulation as well.

The floor inside the dome was slick with bodily fluid and bleach; Brian's feet slapped in the great puddles as he tightened various sections of the wire. His creation was near completion. He would set the stage and show the world what he was made of and they will adore him for it.

And it wouldn't just be the media that would put him on a pedestal.

People all over the world will speak of him in whispers for fear of invoking his spirit. Vigils would be held for the dead by his hand. Pictures will go up on the walls of the dark and curious alike and he would be studied by the greatest minds of the age.

He would be immortalised.

Brian crawled out of the dome, smearing his body with the matter and gore as he wriggled under the net of arms and legs, hands and feet. He bounced with elation over to the DJ both and started flicking all the switched.

Tiny LED of all colours blinked on and the deck lit up with a warm glow. The disco lighting around the room fired up and flashed, a laser came on from above the booth and hit the mass of body parts, its green beam darted and shook over the white of the bleached carrion in waves and patterns. It entranced Brian for a moment and his hand slipped down to stroke his cock under his fiendish apparatus.

For a moment he thought he could hear a car pull up and it snapped him out of his trance. He still had so much to do and was damned if he would be disturbed.

He fingered through a pile of CD's on the decks and picked 'party mix volume 7'.

Sound swamped the hall and the start of 'Club Tropicana' flooded out of the speakers that surrounded the dance floor. Brian started a little celebration dance as he made his way back to the dome to get started with the girls in the middle; if someone had arrived he wouldn't have much time.

Brian slid back under the cage of limbs and got between the two girls. He forcefully pulled up Juicy's head and lined up the copper piping to the opening of the cleaner girl's vaginal opening. He pushed her head down and the makeshift spear entered her.

The cleaner started choking from the pain on the vast dildo that was back in her throat, the end of which was now decorated with the severed fingers of the hotel guests. A flow of saliva pumped past the macabre sex toy as Brian bobbed the Juicy's head up and down.

Brian scooped up a handful of the sludge from the floor and rubbed it over his strap-on and pounded Juicy, poised to thrust into her soft bleached white arsehole. A line of drool left his lips as her arse puckered and twitched with the contact of the cold metal and he licked his lips and pushed.

The semiconscious girl let out a muffled scream behind the headgear as the wall of her anus tore from the metal being forced into her.

It only made Brian push harder.

With each trust of Brian's hips, Juicy's head pushed into the pussy of the cleaner girl, both of the girls shuddering with pain as their body's started to go into shock. Blood poured from between the legs of both girls as 'Copacabana' came out of the speakers.

Brian pulled a tiny remote control from his strap-on and pressed the record button. He had placed a video camera he had found in the prostitute's room above the dome to capture his greatest work, an archive of his genius that would be treasured by the world forever. How they will gasp at his monstrous creation, the living and the dead together in a mass of sexual artistry unrivalled by any know man.

Brian pushed deeper and deeper into the girl's arse and the girl pushed deeper and deeper into the lead girl's pussy; his own cock now rock hard in the corpse pussy stuffed inside his apparatus.

He was so engrossed in his work that he had no recollection of how the bullet passed through his shoulder, a straight in and out after the doors burst open.

The two men were still trying to shoot him as he ripped his way through the dome, causing the wire that was charged with holding crashing. It brought a large section of the celling with it.

He could hear the shots as he ran through a door and into a corridor. He fumbled with the strapping to the crotch spear that was impeding his progress as he fled.

When he got the chance he was going to kill the cunt that shot him.

# 21.

**THE TWO MEN** smashed through the double doors. They were stunned into a halt by what they saw. Jennings couldn't see Biloff's facial expression, but knew it was probably the same as his: a mouth wide open and eyes that were ready to pop free from the skull.

Jennings nearly dropped his gun as he scanned the room. The fucker had built a web out of body parts. Limbs had been roped together with wire and encircled the whole dance floor.

Inside the web a man was fucking a woman whose head looked like it was jammed up a corpse. The girl in the middle was clearly still alive. As she slapped the floor, her blood spurted from between her legs with every rear thrust of the deranged man.

Before he had even realised he had done it Jennings' hand gripped the pistol. He raised it and fired. The gunfire rang out, the sound like cracking trees over the sound of the cheesy pop tunes.

The first two rounds stuck into the limb meat in the web but the third found its mark. It was then that Jennings realised what he was doing.

The man's shoulder burst with red and he looked puzzled for a second then looked up as Biloff joined in with the gunfire.

The freak in the centre of the web fell back pulling with him a huge metal blade from the girl's pussy. It was attached to the man's hips with leather straps. The two women slumped to the ground as the net of limbs gave way and collapsed hulling a part of the roof with it.

Jennings caught a sight of the man slip through a door at the back of the room as the gruesome structure tumbled to the floor.

"Biloff, see to the girls, I'm going after this prick." Jennings burst towards the door, shouting over his shoulder: "And get fucking SWAT here!"

As Jennings clambered over scattered limbs, Biloff started to pull away the web to get to the injured women underneath. With a phone pressed to his ear he screamed for medics and backup.

Jennings shouldered through the swing door the psycho had disappeared through. His gun was poised in front of him, ready to spit fire at the first sign of the bastard. The strap-on from around the killer's waist was in a heap on the floor by his feet. It glistened with gore. Jennings knelt down to inspect it.

He fingered the leather strapping and the images of all of those dead girls hit his mind like he was getting punched. His broken hand thumped with pain once again and he dropped the torturous weapon.

He stiffened up and shook the images from his mind. He pulled his gun back into firing position and continued down the corridor. He checked each door he passed: all of them locked, locked, locked. And then one was unlocked... but it was only a wee broom cupboard.

Every door he passed was either locked or just some small storage room full of clutter until he got to the far end of the corridor and another set of double doors to the kitchen. Jennings quickly looked through one of the round windows and from the brief glimpse the room was clear. Slowly he leaned the door open with his elbow. His gun was the first to enter the room. His eyes darted all around the area then there was a movement to his right.

Before Jennings could swing the gun in the direction on the movement he felt the weight of the shoulder barge and he crashed to the ground. His pistol had caught a corner of one of the stainless steel work stations. He felt a bone in the back of his hand snap. The gun skidded away from him as the murderer took to his feet. Standing over the fallen policeman, the killer smiled in triumph. Then he kicked Jennings full in the face.

Jennings' head bounced off the floor with a crack. He rolled over to try and get to his feet, but it proved daunting, what with two broken hands and all.

The killer howled with delight but Jennings was just about able to roll a fist and swing it. The cartilage in the killer's nose shattered from the perfect right hook, but the man didn't even wince. He just kept on smiling and pushed Jennings back with both hands onto the workstation.

Jennings fell against it awkwardly but returned with another punch to the face, this time right over the eye. The murderer's eye rolled and his head was thrown back so violently that Jennings was sure the bastard had whiplash. A chop from the broken left hand to the neck, another right hook to the jaw, and he had gone beyond the pain. The killer's legs buckled for a split second.

He had the fucker now.

With the scent of victory in his nostrils Jennings rolled over the man, wrapping his arm around his throat and wedging it in his other arm wrapped around the back of the killer's head.

"You're going to sleep, fucker!"

The killer's eye's bulged and his teeth ground down hard. He exhaled hard sending a jet of blood and snot down his chin and he put his hand back to find the officer's eye socket with his thumb.

Jennings screamed as the bony thumb dug deep and everything went red. His grip slipped and the killer grabbed at his left arm. Before Jennings knew what was happening the murderer had sunk his teeth into the damaged, bandaged had.

Jennings was now fully back at home with the pain.

He tried to pull his hand away but the killer had locked his jaw up. He shook his head like a pit-bull with a mouth full of busted thumb. The pain was so terrible Jennings couldn't even scream. But then the pressure was off and he rolled back onto the floor clutching his mangled hand.

Then the first of the heavy blows came crashing down on him.

The killer had a fire extinguisher and struck Jennings square in the centre of his forehead. With a blinding white flash of shock, his brain collided with the inner wall of his skull.

There was another swing of the heavy canister on the side of his head and another flash like lightning. Images of the women from the forensic pictures slowly ebbing away into the ether as another flash of white sent him closer to the abyss.

For a moment Jennings thought he was smiling.

Flash, flash, flash...

... Then nothing.

## 22.

MICHAEL SAT IN his car with his head in his hands. He was not quite able to digest what he was seeing.

The hotel car park was now a full on SWAT operation with lines of cars and armed officers circling the building. Floodlights had been set up along with operations tents and communication wagons.

The press had turned up too.

Cameramen jostled to get the best shot as news readers fixed their hair and dusted the dandruff from the shoulders from their bespoke suits.

It was then he realised that he was sitting in the nude. That he was covered in vomit, with a raging hard-on, and stuck quite in the middle of a media frenzy come potential warzone.

He pulled his shirt over his lap and slowly reversed out of the car park onto the country lane slip road that ran off of the motorway. The hotel was surrounded by several small lakes. Michael pulled into an adjacent field to wash in one of them, parking his beat up old car behind a hedge row and effectively out of sight.

The lake was well out of the way of the hotel but Michael could still hear the hubbub from the car park. Still clutching his shirt to save his embarrassment he hopped across the field and into the violently cold water of the lake to clean up.

As soon as the chilled water washed over him he felt calm, a peace from the comedown of the blood spirit. He floated on his back for a while, drifting out to the centre of the lake. His cock was still hard and sticking out like a mast.

Michael flicked at his engorged penis and splashed water over his groin. He dipped his head under the water to blow bubbles from his nose. He was far too busy emptying his lungs with his head submerged to see the farmer coming across the field to investigate the trespasser skinny dipping in his lake.

The farmer was shouting but with his ears full of water and his mind full of images of the dismembered girl left in his flat, he didn't hear a thing. It wasn't until the farmer threw a rock into the water where Michael was floating that he grabbed his attention.

"What the bloody hell do you think you are doing?" The famers face had gone bright red like a cartoon fat man. "If you want a swim, piss off down to the local baths."

Michael started to doggy paddle his way back to the edge of the lake, his own blood boiling from being disturbed. The audacity of the man bothered him but Michael would have to keep his cool. What with all the police less than five hundred yards away.

"So sorry," Michael heaved out of the water and covered his shame with both hands, "it was just so hot and the water looked so inviting, I couldn't help myself."

The farmer seemed to calm when confronted by such a scrawny nerd. "Well it's no harm done I guess, but get off with you, and don't come back down here."

"Oh, don't worry I won't be back this way." And with that Michael lunged at the man, wrapping his arms and legs around the farmer and falling back into the water.

The two men rolled under the water with the farmer grasping for the surface as Michael squeezed the air from his lungs like a serpent; tighter and tighter until the farmer could do nothing but gulp down a mouthful of water into his lungs.

With the liquid burning away in his lungs the fight soon fell away from the man as his brain was starved of oxygen. His flailing arms began to slow. Michael sensed the kill and put all his might into his arms bending the farmer's neck almost in half. The water amplified the satisfying crack as the neck snapped and the farmer fell still in his arms.

Michaels breathing was shallow as he pulled the body on to the bank; he looked at the corpse with the awkward angle in its neck then over to his car. Lot of blood in the big man, a lot of blood he could use as well as a change of clothes no matter if they were just track suit bottoms and a t-shirt, no matter how wet they were.

He stripped the farmer down and climbed into his oversized track pants. He pulled the drawstring tight and tied it into a bow. Then Michael slipped into the soggy trainers and t-shirt. The clothes hung on him like wet sheets. The shoes squelched as he dragged the dead farmer across the thick grass to the boot of his car.

The man must have been twice his size but he could still lift him into the back of the car with ease. The residual effect of the blood spirit was still working its magic.

Michael sat on the bonnet of the car for a while, the warm evening air drying his new baggy clothes as he assessed the situation. He would have to get into the hotel somehow. He would have to get to the killer before the police killed got all gung-ho and shot him to bits in the car park.

His thoughts were shattered by the sound of two gun shots ringing out over the field. Michael nearly fell off the bonnet of the car turning so quickly towards the hotel.

*Was it all over?*

He slid off the car and hurried towards the country road. He didn't want to risk taking the car back to the hotel with a corpse in the boot and the place crawling with police. He had his morgue ID in his wallet just in case any officers asked him any questions. He could make something up on the spot or just kill them. The blame would probably land on the killer in the hotel if there weren't any witnesses.

The trainers were wet and a good couple of sizes too big. They slapped and squelched on the road as he jogged towards the cop heavy crime scene. One that was by now on red alert due to the shootings.

And so with wallet in hand and pulling the baggy tracksuit bottoms up Michael bounded down the country lane towards the hotel and what could easily be the most important thing he was ever to do in his life.

But that was just fine with Michael. He felt so alive.

# 23.

WITH THE CONTENTS of the policeman's head now splattered up him, Brian ducked through a side door into another part of the dining area. It was a serving hatch between the kitchen and the canteen like eating hall.

He would have to deal with the other cop. He was sure to find his partner sooner or later lying in the hallway, folded up like a wet beach towel. Then he would come with a belly full of anger and a pistol primed just for him.

Brian's cock was still hard as he spread the congealing blood over his chest, picking off the clots and sucking them like boiled sweets as he made his way through the dining room. He kept low, ducking from table to table waiting for the first of the policeman's shots to be thrown his way; but they didn't come.

Maybe he had his hands full with the two girls left in the heap of limbs on the dance floor. Those fucking cops had ruined his installation, turning up as they did at just the exact wrong moment.

Brian was glad he'd killed the first cop and was rather looking forward to killing the second. So much so that his penis was jutting out like a pan handle.

Through another door and into what could only been the cleaners break area. Posters of half-naked women covered the wall and the place stank with disinfectant and vomit.

Brian slumped against the wall out of breath and took his swollen member into his hand and jerked it hard. It was a matter of moments before a jet of jizum splashed against the side of a dirty grey locker.

He ran the blood and semen covered hand over his face and inhaled deeply, the scent sending his head into a spin as the door to the break room burst open.

The other cop bolted into the room with his gun raised out in front of him but he had rushed in too far, overcommitted, and passed the still panting killer by the lockers.

Brian jumped on the larger man in a frenzy of biting and scratching, his body slapped against the policeman's as the pair slammed to the ground. The policeman's gun slipped from his grip and spun about on his finger like a cowboy performing gun tricks.

The two men struggled on the ground as Brian sunk his teeth into a soft part of the cop's face. Sickly blood flooded into his mouth and he jerked his head back taking a lump of skin with him. The cop underneath him screamed and got a hold of his pistol and tried to roll away from his attacker.

A row of police cars had gathered at the front of the hotel. Black vans had also arrived and a SWAT team had assembled under a makeshift tent in the middle of the car park. A platform had gone up and two marksmen set up shop high over the hubbub below.

Important men in uniform pointed at stuff. Less important men buzzed around following orders. The even less important men help back up the lines of reporters and camera crews at the entrance to the car park.

The place was a zoo.

Then a muffled gunshot from inside the building made everything freeze. All eyes were on the eerily silent hotel. Just the crackled words of panic over radios could be heard, "What's happening, god damnit! Someone? Anyone?"

Nothing moved, nothing was said, a hush over the whole area, waiting for anything to happen.

Two more sudden shots sent the car park into frenzy as if a giant had dropped an ant farm. Officers of all ranks swarmed over each other and the reporters surged into the car park as the line of police broke.

Chaos ensued.

Members of the SWAT team fell over each other to get into position at the front of the hotel. The officers pointing at stuff earlier pointed with even more vigour to the point of frantic. People screaming on phones and over radios drowned out the live reports being filmed as reporters flicked their hair and wiped donut crumbs from their tailored suits as they went live.

Then the shout went up from one of the marksmen on the raised platform:

"THE ROOF, THERE'S SOMETHING HAPPENING ON THE ROOF!"

Brian pushed the wounded policeman through the door to at the top of the stairs by his head with a hollow thud. The lump of an officer was half dead and staggering. His own gun pressed hard into his back.

The gnarly strap-on now back on Brian's hips bumped against Biloff's striped backside.

Blood pulsed from the bullet wounds in the stomach of the limping police man, down his legs leaving red footprints on the warm felted roof. Brian forced him towards the ledge and the waiting audience below for the finale of his greatest work.

Unblinking he bent the officer over the walled ledge to face the crowd. He angled up the tip of the jagged copper dick over his bloody arsehole. The crowd held its breath as the

109

maniac plunged his hips into the exposed rump of the prone detective on the roof.

A rush of shitty blood gushed up Brian's belly as he fucked the copper into oblivion. Churning away Brian was turning the cop's intestines to mush. The detective belched out his pulped innards like a waterfall down the side of the building.

Below a police constable turned to be sick into his hat.

Brian screamed with delight and fired the gun into the air in triumph as the marksmen on the raised platform tickled at the triggers of their high calibre weapons.

As Biloff coughed the last of his mashed up guts and life down the wall two pops from the raised platform turned Brian's head into a fountain of blood, brain and splintered skull. His body seized up, flicking the copper tube strap-on out from between the legs of the dead policeman, sending the body falling limply to the ground and into a final heap.

Michael looked on in amazement at the event. He couldn't believe his eyes as he watched the body fall to the ground and the killer's head burst as two rounds of high powered ammunition crashed into their target.

His hands came up to his mouth with the cold realisation of what was happening. The secret to the blood spirit had just exploded on the roof of a cheap hotel. All that he had done to get to this moment was for nothing. Without his hands holding up his soggy tracksuit bottoms they slipped to the ground and he began to cry.

It was over.

There was a dead farmer in a pond, a dead kid outside a corner shop and a chopped up woman in his bath and he had nothing to show for it. He had gone on a rampage for no reason but his own greed. His heart sank in his chest.

In all of the commotion happening in the car park no one notices a man with his pants around his ankles weeping.

For the first time in a long time he felt completely hopeless.

## End.

## ABOUT THE AUTHOR:

Gregor Cole works out of Kent (the garden of England) in the UK spending most of his free time scribbling away in the gloom and watching classic horror.
He sharpens the knives of his craft on a diet of tea, biscuits and lemon loaf cake, constantly waiting for the postman to deliver his weekly selection of gore films and Bizarro literature.

Also available from ~MorbidbookS~

In Print & Kindle Editions:

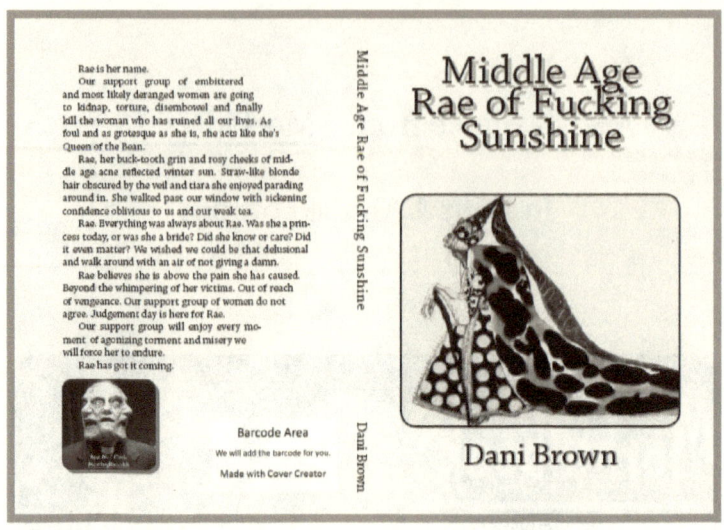

Rae is her name.

Our support group of embittered and most likely deranged women are going to kidnap, torture, disembowel and finally kill the woman who has ruined all our lives. As foul and as grotesque as she is, she acts like she's Queen of the Bean.

Rae, her buck-tooth grin and rosy cheeks of middle age acne reflected winter sun. Straw-like blonde hair obscured by the veil and tiara she enjoyed parading around in. She walked past our window with sickening confidence oblivious to us and our weak tea.

Rae believes she is above the pain she has caused. Beyond the whimpering of her victims. Out of reach of vengeance. Our support group of women do not agree. Judgement day is here for Rae.

Rae has got it coming.

"No! You will not move. You say I am a fucking clown, and so I will be. And I will fuck you until I can fuck you no more. And when I am done, perhaps I will take you down to the cattle car and watch while the other clowns fuck you one by one until you are so full that their juices run down your thighs. You will learn to show respect for me. For my art and my craft."

Pinning her hands to the bed, he entered her quickly and roughly. She screamed and spit in his face. He slapped her again and left her ear ringing as he wiped the spittle from her face and continued to pound her hard and fast.

"You hate clowns? Well you have a clown inside of you right now. How does that feel? A fucking clown is raping you and he'll continue to do it until it pleases him to stop."

~The hands of the girls were inside of each-others zip front grey boiler suits and they sat in the blood from where Sonny's face collided with the surface. The brunette had a finger smear of it next to her mouth.

"You two sluts put each other down and go tell Moira that Sonny's done. I'm coming in, just got a little business to attend to first."

As the two started to leave the big blond grabbed the shoulder of the red head and pulled her back.

"Not you Fire-Crotch, all this fucking blood has got me going." She started to unbuckle the belt on her camouflage hot pants.

"Down you go, bitch!"

~Short stories from the Most Depraved Writer in Print. Dark and twisted tales of exquisite violence, rough tricks, narcotics consumption, evil ghosts and drug-snuffling demons. Evil grandfathers and animal-human hybrid clones. Morbid serial killer stalking night darkened hallways of an unsuspecting hospital. Life underground following the frozen apocalypse. Tales of ancient blood-thirsty vampires and Roman decadence. Enjoy all of the hardcore, dystopic, viscerally violent stories. Not for easily offended mamby-pambies. Dark fiction at its finest.

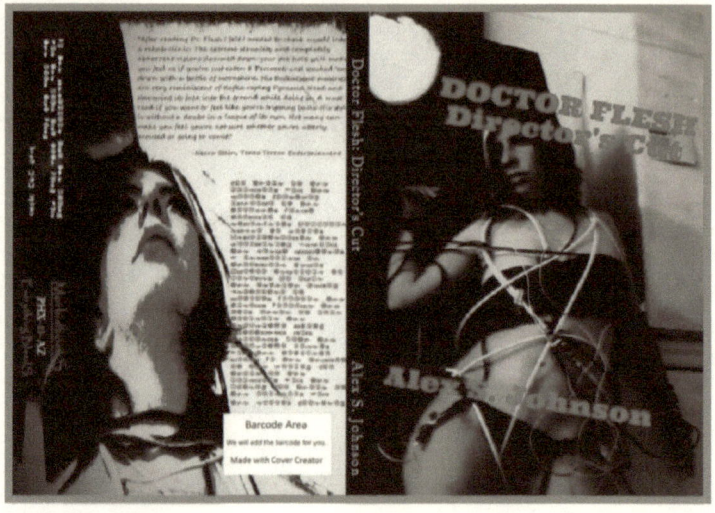

~From Alex S. Johnson, the author of Bad Sunset, Wicked Candy and The Death Jazz, comes a new vision in Bizarro horror. Imagine a TROMA film on meth and acid, one part cyberpunk, one part Franz Kafka, and three parts frankly unsuitable for a sane audience. "Will make you feel as if you've just eaten 8 Percocets and washed 'em down with a bottle of moonshine," says Necro Stein of Texas Terror Entertainment.

~**When the winds blew i felt them blowing through me,** when the land shook, it was my corpus that trembled. When the tides ebbed and flowed I became more shore and more sea. I was day and night as the sun and moon described the steps of their dancing within me. Just as I could see all the world at once, I was all of these things at once, and the motion of an entire world formed the foundation of my stillness.

I'd travelled through the Sphere of Glammeth, descended through the Guardian, and then through the Grey-Man, fallen through a hole that pierced all the worlds.

~**He had to have her the moment he saw her trachea ring**. Six months later she was his lovely wife. He performed his duties as a husband and she as a wife. He tolerated a house filled with references to her late first husband and the children they had together. He put up with her prudish ways. He waited. He was patient. He planned. He was adaptable. He was rewarded over the course of a week in her basement. He turned his perverse sexual fantasies of worms and maggots and her lovely crusty trachea ring into a gruesome reality.

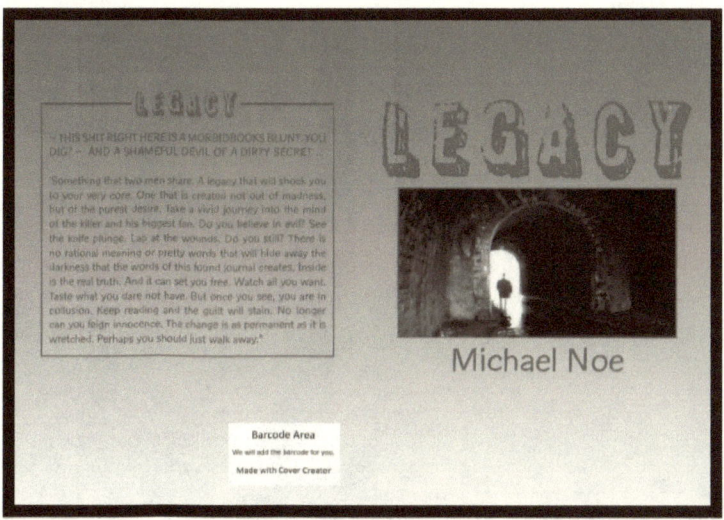

## ~A dirty shameful devil of a secret...

Something that two men share. A legacy that will shock you to your very core. One that is created not out of madness, but of the purest desire. Take a vivid journey into the mind of the killer and his biggest fan. Do you believe in evil? See the knife plunge. Lap at the wounds. Do you still? There is no rational meaning or pretty words that will hide away the darkness that the words of this found journal creates. Inside is the real truth. And it can set you free. Watch all you want. Taste what you dare not have.

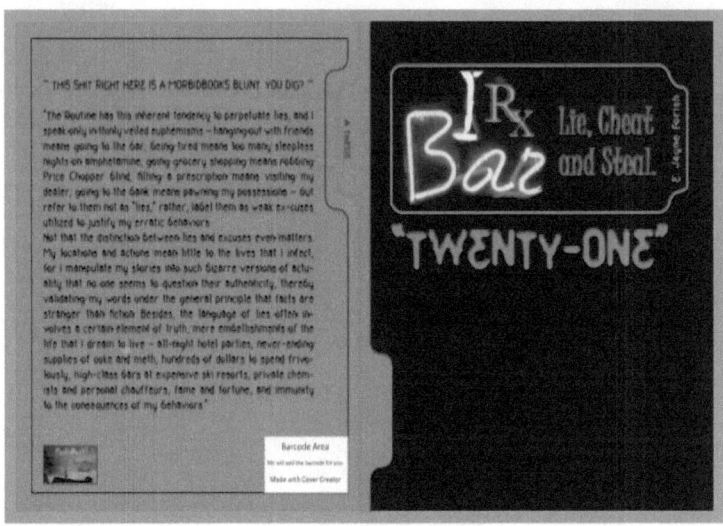

~"**The routine has this inherent tendency to perpetuate lies,** and I speak only in thinly veiled euphemisms — hanging out with friends means going to the bar; being tired means too many sleepless nights on amphetamine; going grocery shopping means robbing Price Chopper blind; filling a prescription means visiting my dealer; going to the bank means pawning my possessions — but refer to them not as "lies;" rather, label them as weak excuses utilized to justify my erratic behaviours.

~**I'm feeling down and dirty, feeling kind of mean,** so I give those fans my middle finger. Those poor bastards go nuts. My team looks at me in awe. My coach frowns and the opposing one begins to furiously scratch out new plays. I see our opponents and I almost feel sorry for the poor bastards. Their fans can't help them. Their coach can't help them. I'm going to run them off their own track in front of their own fans and there is not one thing they can do about it.

~**Humanity is the devil is a deconstructed nightmare mixing David Lynch and snuff movies.** The plot revolves around a central character, Seth, who is set about a crusade against humanity which, for him, represents pure evil. Through random killings he and his cronies try to accelerate the end of the world, in order to provoke and defeat the Demiurge, the false God that is ruling the earth. As in Burroughs, logical language is replaced here with cut-scenes – sometimes to be taken literally – that plunge the reader into an extreme experience.

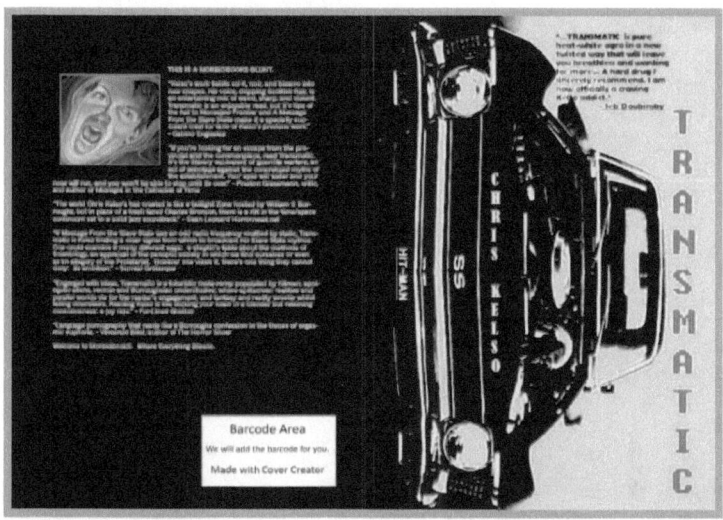

~"As a part-time hitman/ exterminator, Ignius Ellis's dream is to buy a candy-apple red Nova Supreme. In the process of trying to earn enough cash to make his dream come true he gets sucked into the rough world of Visitacion Valley, SF. When the tenants in his apartment complex reveal their various extracurricular activities this take an even more bizarre twist and Ellis soon becomes acquainted with the nightmarish Slave State dimension..."

## ~That's the last time she gets the bigger worm...

Once their flesh flakes away the angels collapse into puddles of hissing goop and withered petals blow into them hurried along by unseen winds. My spit looses its sweet taste to the black flavor of ash. The glowing birds in the bright orange sky burst into small sparkly novas. The sky itself weeps and tears, streaking down like a ruined painting as the dismal grey of life wheezes back before my eyes. I don't blink; praying silently for one last desperate sensation of the high. Lila feels it too. She writhes on the mattress next to me…

~Scary as ever.

He looked at her and grinned wickedly, the overcasting shadows of the outer corner of the stone wall, combined with the flickering light above them, created a deadly feature across the side of his face. He sees her lying helpless. He chuckled eerily, and instantly raised his hand. Her eyes widened to the sight of the gleaming sharp knife in his grasp. He even held it up for her to see it better.

She stared up at him and then to the knife, panting in fear. Her heart pounded throughout her body as he chuckled once more saying deeply,

"Oh excellent. I've found you . . ."

~**Within these twisted and perverted pages**, Johnson manages to demolish clichés with a jaded finesse that I've personally never encountered in written form. Another apparent talent is his effortless deconstruction of pop-culture allegories and references as found in his story "Vampussy." No one is safe or spared from his dagger sharp sarcasm and wit.

While not without its flaws, my appreciation for this kind of talent and voice is what made his writing so fun to read, even if he might possibly be out of his ever-loving mind.

~In Garrett Cook's Murderland serial killers are idolized by society. Their deeds are followed obsessively by television pundits and the adoring public. A subculture has grown up around this phenomena, called "Reap." Laws are created to allow this activity to flourish, including designated "safe zones' where killers can practice their trade without fear of persecution. Fans of the top rated serial killers celebrate each new kill on social media and television. Programs glorify their deeds.

The culture of Murderland is violent and mirrors our own violent society and its decadent obsessions.

~Born whole from the rectum of a dying patient, Morbid silently stalks the hospital's hallways, heinously dispatching the most helpless of patients and in the most painfully repulsive of manners. In the meantime, in order to pay for his family and home that includes his ghost step-father Sammy and his pet aborted fetus Chip, Westphal has to ingest mounds of dangerous narcotics to get through his night shifts. Barely hanging on to his Care Tech gig by his fingernails, the last thing Westphal needs is to be accused of Morbid's evil deeds. You, on the other hand, simply seek some solace from all Your diseases.

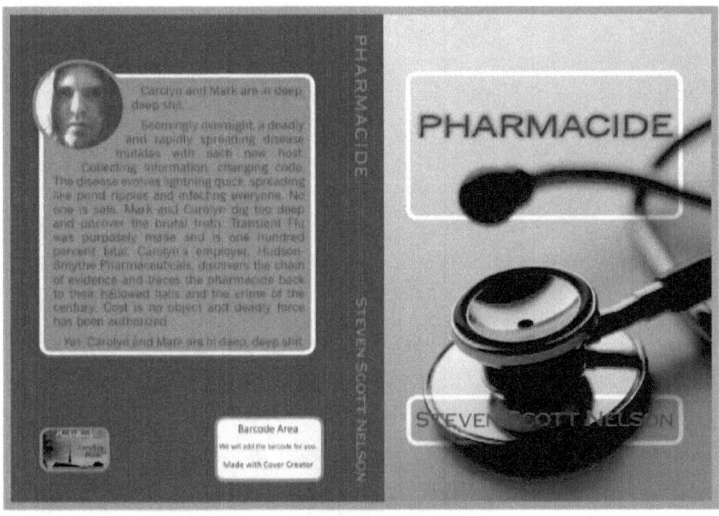

~**It looks like Carolyn and Mark are in deep, deep shit...** Mark and Carolyn live in an alternate 1989 where Ronald Reagan is on his fourth presidential term. The USA has a rigid, long-standing caste system and abortions were never made legal. Being homeless is a crime that is punishable by imprisonment in Tent City. Most of Mark's ER patients are inmates at this camp and are victims of a new disease dubbed: Transient Flu. This deadly and rapidly spreading disease mutates with each new host, collecting information, changing code. The disease evolves lightning quick, spreading like pond ripples...

~IMMANUEL THE CHRIST **has some nerve.** Jonah has already lost everyone he loves to Pilate the vampire and his Harbor drug violence. Jonah now trudges through his days staying as high on Plata as possible. He just wants to be left alone while he waits for his turn to die. The Christ has other plans for him. She sends Pedro, to assign Jonah to order the Herod to dismantle the Harbor's Plata trade. Jonah decides to run. But you can't run from God. As Jonah learns the hard way when the 'Edmund Fitzgerald' goes down in rough seas, with the reluctant prophet on board...

Dig this: The fictional world of Reverend Rage contains graphic violence, illicit drug use, non-consensual extreme sex, and potentially offensive material given the religious references. It is intended for grown folks. Other than that, you are sure to dig the Reverend's sample lines. You know, try out a gram before you commit to an 8-ball. Aren't you the clever goose...

"Rage writes with his conscience thrown out the window."
—Nick Cato

THE GRIM REVEREND

RAGE PRIMER
WICKED SHORTS

REVEREND STEVEN RAGE

Barcode Area
We will add the barcode for you.
Made with Cover Creator

**~Five Very Wicked Shorts**. Brought to you with love and blood from The Grim Reverend Steven Rage, the 'Most Depraved Writer in Print'. ~

Through the sheer shock of his presentation, Rage forces readers to consider the alternatives, to look at the garbage in the streets, to see what is swept into the gutters at night right before all decent people awake to see another cleaned up version of the day. Depravity at its finest, but really the stories are loads of fun.

~Pontius Pilate is cursed to be a vampire. Life after life after life.~ And for the Plata dealing Pilate, his life is more like a death sentence. His only chance surviving is to keep on selling his monthly quota of Plata. This new man-made narcotic is a potent speed-ball designed to amp up the user, while also numbing the conscience into euphoric oblivion. To nullify the pain. To stifle the torture. To run and to hid from all the anguish inside. PILATE is a drug lord vampire in this re-telling of Christ's final days.

~**So I, The Spun Monkey, have returned from running my errands, safe and sound.** Having failed rehab once again, The Spun Monkey went ahead and procured myself an 8-ball of crispy, crunchy Columbian Bam-Bam. I chipped, chopped, lined and blasted off with two bigguns up each side. OOH OOH EEE EEE-fuckmerunning- OOH-OOH-OOH, motherfuckers! Monkey be ready... Yes, indeeeeeed.... Having had my jet fuel, I then sat my hairy asshole down at the keyboard and began flailing away. The monkey hopes you dig the fruits of my labors in 'The Spun Monkey's Digest'. And if you not ... well then ... you can go eff yourself, Capitan!

~**Following religious folklore, parables, and beliefs,** Rage presents the readers with a God who truly is the Shepherd that leaves no sheep behind. While this tale is deeply woven with the intricacies of a dark, drug-infested world ruled by evil forces, this is the story of a lost sheep. All are God's children, even the most foulest of evil creatures who by their own will have become so through their spiritual and physical copulation with the Devil, and as such, in God's mercy, still are given a chance to be saved.

~ CARGO CONTAINS: ~

Space-wrecked on Venus by Neil R. Jones

For All the Marbles by Rev. Steven Rage

Tony and the Beetles by Philip K. Dick

Acid Bath by Vaseleos Garson

The Butterfly Kiss by Arthur Dekker Savage

The Moon Destroyers by Monroe K. Ruch

From some of the giants of the Golden Age to the darkest of
dystopian noir, MorbidbookS SciFi Anthology will take you from
hopeful space travel to living hand-to-mouth in the despair
beneath the Earth.

Welcome to your future.

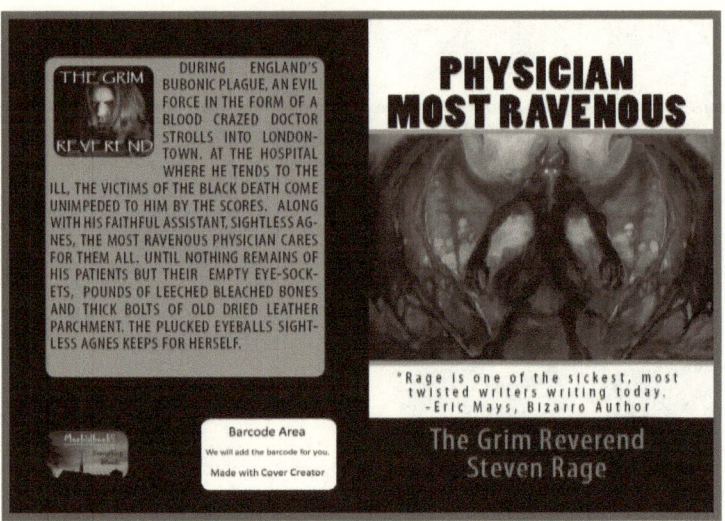

~During the height of England's Bubonic Plague an ancient Evil Force strolls into London-Town in the form of a would-be doctor. It could smell the blood from miles away, wanting only to help. At the hospital where he cares for the victims of this Black Death, the ill come to him unimpeded. They arrived and fell by the scores. With the help of his ever-faithful assistant, Sightless Agnes, a most ravenous cares for them all. Eating his way through an entire hospital, he treats them until there is nothing left. Nothing save their empty eye sockets, a few pounds of leeched bleached bones and some bolts of old dried-out flesh-leather parchment.

**~New from MorbidbookS; Where Everything Bleeds** is an instant collector's specimen and a certain stunner. ~ Be the first freak on your block to acquire this singular and unexpurgated exquisite culling of The Grim Reverend Steven Rage's favorite 'meds'. Enjoy this one-of-a-kind vivid look into the twisted mind of The Most Depraved Writer In Print as he captains you through the intoxicating stain of his wicked imagination. Included are numerous Photos, Paintings and Illustrations embellished with dramatic grayscale that enhance these iniquitous and magnificent Dark Fantasy fables.

MorbidbookS. Everything Bleeds.